FERALS

THE WHITE WIDOW'S REVENGE

FERALS

THE WHITE WIDOW'S REVENGE

BY JACOB GREY

HARPER

An Imprint of HarperCollinsPublishers

Library of Congress Control Number: 2016949911

ISBN 978-0-06-232109-1 (trade bdg.)

Typography by Sarah Creech

16 17 18 19 20   CG/RRDH   10 9 8 7 6 5 4 3 2 1

❖

First Edition

With special thanks to Michael Ford

1

They've got no idea, thought Caw. *No idea how much danger they're in.*

He pulled up his collar, even though he was already soaked to the skin, and looked out across the street. It was quiet because of the awful weather, but a few people still went about their business. A man in a dark suit ate a sandwich under a dripping canopy. Cars swished across the slick road. A boy holding hands with his mother rushed into a shoe shop to get out of the downpour.

It had been raining for days, but the low gray clouds showed no signs of being empty. The streets were saturated, and puddles dotted the rooftop on which Caw stood. He looked down at the secondhand sneakers he'd found at a clothing bank. Water had long ago seeped through the fabric, and his toes squelched, but he'd been wet through enough times in his life that it didn't really bother him. Growing up in the nest in Blackstone Park, he'd seen many storms blow through the city and rip the tarpaulin cover loose. If they couldn't fix it, Caw and his crows just huddled down, lashed by the wind and rain. He had hated it, but he always knew it would pass.

I've forgotten what the sun looks like, said Screech. The youngest of Caw's crows was sitting on the roof parapet with his feathers puffed out to protect him from the rain. The other two birds perched beside him.

Maybe we should go home, said Glum hopefully. His beak rested on his chest and his eyes were shut.

Shimmer cocked her head. *Quit complaining,* she said. *A bit of water won't do you any harm.*

To anyone in the street below, the three crows would have looked completely unremarkable, Caw thought. But then, nobody but a feral would realize he could understand what they were saying.

"Crumb wants us to wait here while he checks out the bank," said Caw, nodding at the building across the street.

There are twenty banks in Blackstone, said Glum. *The chances of them hitting this one are pretty slim.*

Caw shrugged.

I can go down and take a look if you want, said Shimmer, hopping restlessly.

Caw thought about it. Their enemies could be down below, and if they saw a crow acting strangely, it might spook them.

He wondered if he should send Shimmer to the hospital

instead, to peer in at a window and check on Selina. At least that would give her something to do. She would obey him, though she wasn't exactly crazy about the daughter of the Mother of Flies. No one was, really, apart from Caw. But Selina Davenport was in the hospital because of him—she had taken a bullet to save his life.

In the two weeks since the battle on top of Commissioner Davenport's apartment, Selina had lain unconscious in a Blackstone Hospital bed. The doctors didn't know why she wasn't waking up. They thought it might be some sort of infection. Caw's friend Crumb, the pigeon feral, said it might be better if she *never* woke up. Caw couldn't reply to that. Despite what everyone else thought, Selina was his friend too. She'd stuck by him when it mattered most.

Hello? said Shimmer. *What do you say, boss? I can scan the block. No one will even see me.*

"Okay," said Caw. "Just be careful."

Shimmer took off, spreading her wings in a low glide and dipping out of sight. Caw would ask Glum to take on hospital duty later. Any day now, there must be good news.

He heard a squeak and turned to see Pip, the young mouse feral, and the lanky Crumb climbing up from the fire escape.

About time, said Glum.

Crumb was holding aloft a battered umbrella, and Pip stayed close to his side as they hurried across the roof.

A pigeon landed with a clumsy hop beside Crumb.

"Keep watch, Bobbin," said the pigeon feral. Despite the umbrella, his brown hair lay in wet straggles across his forehead and his scruffy beard was beaded with water. "This is the place."

Caw looked across the street at the ornate three-story facade of the Blackstone Savings Bank.

"How do you know?" he said. "Everything looks normal."

"Turns out the manager is a feral," said Pip eagerly. The mouse talker's eyes were eager saucers under the hood of his waterproof jacket. It was at least three sizes too big and came down to his knees.

Crumb nodded. "Pickwick—the sparrow talker. That's probably why the escaped convicts chose it—they get the money, plus they hit back at the ferals who are trying to stop them."

Caw's heart began to beat faster. He knew how ruthless their enemies were. A few weeks ago, the Mother of Flies had released Blackstone's most dangerous convicts and turned them into an army of new ferals, using the power of the Midnight Stone. She had given each of them an animal species to control in return for doing her bidding.

Caw might have defeated the commissioner on the apartment rooftop, but her ferals were still on the loose. Crime had been on the rise across the city, made a hundred times worse by the convicts' new feral powers. Thefts, assaults, vandalism . . . The papers had picked up a few odd stories about animals at the scenes of crimes—a colony of vultures swooping over the town hall, an infestation of raccoons at a movie theater—but the police hadn't made the connection. Caw couldn't blame them—they had no idea ferals existed.

That morning a casino break-in had left two security guards dead, with lacerations to their throats—the work of Lugmann, the new panther feral. It was sheer luck that a couple of Pip's mice had been at the scene and had overheard the plan to hit a bank.

Caw clenched his fists. As the convicts mastered their feral powers, they would only become more deadly. They had to be stopped.

"Should we let the others know?" Caw asked. Mrs. Strickham and the other good ferals were positioned all across Blackstone, watching the banks.

Crumb shook his head. "There's still a chance they'll hit a different bank. I'm afraid this one's on us."

"And Pickwick's ready?" said Caw, glancing down to his weapon, the Crow's Beak. The short, black-bladed sword of the crow line hung at Caw's side, in a sheath he'd made from the remains of an old leather satchel.

"Pickwick's not a fighter," Crumb said. "He rarely even speaks to his birds anymore. But he'll get any innocent bystanders out of the way."

Caw found it strange to think of a feral not using his powers.

Just living a normal life. Nothing about Caw's life had ever been normal.

Shimmer swooped up with an urgent squawk.

They're coming! she said. *Black van, five blocks east, stopped at the lights.*

"Good work," said Caw. He turned to Crumb and Pip. "They're almost here."

Crumb waved an arm, and several pigeons flocked to him from surrounding buildings. Pip leaned over the edge of the roof. Caw heard a scream in the street below and looked down to see a young girl scramble into her mother's arms. A wriggling surge of mice had emerged from a drain and poured over the road as passersby backed away.

Pip grinned. "Who needs a panther when you've got a mouse or two?"

With a flick of his hand, he directed the horde of mice up the steps of the bank. The mass of their bodies was enough to open the automatic doors, and they swept through. Screaming customers ran out, and a moment later a small gray-haired man in a suit and glasses followed, muttering apologies. He looked up to the roof and gave a small salute.

Crumb nodded back. "Let's get down there."

"Fetch the others," Caw said to Screech, and the crows took off as he sprinted to the fire escape. Adrenaline coursed through

Caw's veins as he took the rails in both hands and slid down, his heels slamming into the platform below. He ran to the next stairs and did the same, reaching ground level in seconds. Then he darted across the street. What with the plague of mice and the bad weather, the sidewalks were almost empty.

Mr. Pickwick saw Caw coming and squinted. "Sorry, closing early," he said. "Vermin infestation."

"I'm the crow talker," said Caw urgently. They had to get inside before the convicts' van arrived.

The old man looked him up and down suspiciously.

"He's with me," said a voice from above. Crumb and Pip were hovering in the rain, held by several dozen pigeons.

Mr. Pickwick smiled grimly as they landed in front of him. "I stand corrected. Come in, quickly."

The bank was old-fashioned, with wooden counters embossed with bronze plating and a huge mural of swirling oil colors on one wall. The air smelled of floor polish, and the only sounds were the scuffing of footsteps as Mr. Pickwick's staff hurried out through the back offices.

"How do we lock the doors?" said Caw, looking at the glass panels behind them.

"There's a switch—bottom left," said Mr. Pickwick.

Caw found the switch under a clear plastic hood and pressed it. The thick glass doors glided shut.

"The glass is bulletproof," said Mr. Pickwick.

"Call the police on the hotline," said Crumb.

As the bank manager picked up the phone from a counter, a black van screeched to a halt beside the steps outside, making Caw's heart jolt. He recognized the driver's crew-cut hair and his muscular arms blue with prison tattoos. *Lugmann.* The convict's eyes widened as he leaned over to look into the bank and saw Caw. He grinned crookedly. Caw grabbed the hilt of his sword.

The back doors of the van burst open and a woman with a shaved head and a pierced lip jumped out. Caw remembered her from the fight on the commissioner's roof. She beckoned to *something* in the van.

The van's suspension dipped and a giant head peered out. A huge bison sniffed the air, then stomped down to the sidewalk. The sheer size of it made Caw's knees turn to liquid—its hooves were the size of dinner plates. Its head swayed toward them, and it gave a guttural bellow as strings of drool dripped from its mouth.

"Is the door bison-proof?" asked Crumb, his face pale. They stood transfixed as the enormous beast lumbered up the steps, snorting through flaring nostrils.

Lugmann stepped out of the van, a large, sleek black cat following at his heels. He looked up and down the street and then straight at Caw. He put his hands together as if in prayer, then moved them

8

apart, mouthing, "Open the door." Caw shook his head.

The shaven-headed woman commanded the bison, and the creature charged forward, slamming headfirst into the door with a huge *crash*.

Everyone jumped back. The glass shook but didn't break. The bison backed up, then charged once more. The glass held, but the metal door hinges were twisting out of shape.

"They must have cut the line," said Mr. Pickwick, holding the phone limply. "It's dead. Does anyone have a cell phone?"

Crumb shook his head.

Caw's heart sank. But he pushed his fear aside and let his mind reach out, searching for his crows. Clenching his fists, he drew the birds toward him.

Through the glass, he saw a black cloud swoop down from the surrounding buildings.

Get the bison! He sent a murder of crows at the creature, and others broke off and attacked the female feral with their talons. Her hold on the bison must have been severed as she flailed under the assault of the black birds, because the huge beast staggered back down the steps and thumped into the side of the van.

Lugmann appeared through the flock of birds, wielding a sledgehammer. As he reached the top of the steps, he swung it at the glass doors. The impact reverberated through the bank, making

Pickwick jump. Lugmann took a step back and swung again, throwing all his weight behind the hammer. A few cracks appeared in the glass. Then Crumb's pigeons joined the fight, smacking into Lugmann as he hefted the hammer again. He tried to shake them off, but more swarmed over him. He dropped the sledgehammer and retreated to the van, tugging his accomplice inside with him and slamming the door behind them.

"Goodness," said Pickwick. "Are we . . . Is it over?"

The grunts of the bison were muted through the glass. Lugmann and the feral woman were trapped in the van by the crows and pigeons, staring out with cold malice. Surely someone outside had called the police by now.

But Caw's heart refused to slow down. *It can't be this easy. . . .*

"We did it," said Crumb.

"Not quite," said a familiar southern drawl.

Caw flinched and spun around. The oil-painted mural that covered one wall was shifting in a way that made his eyes strain and blink. Then the shape of a man emerged, the colors of his suit flickering before settling into pale cream. It was Mr. Silk, the moth feral. He tipped his broad-brimmed hat.

"Mighty nice of you to join me, Caw."

Caw flung out a hand, but all his crows were still outside. He glanced at Crumb, but the pigeon feral had made the same mistake.

"Who are you?" asked Pickwick.

"Just a customer, come to make a withdrawal," said Mr. Silk. "A substantial one."

"Pip, get him!" yelled Caw.

A surge of mice flooded toward the moth feral, but Mr. Silk only looked bored as he raised both arms. The walls and ceiling came alive. Thousands of moths peeled from every surface, burying the mice in seconds and flooding Caw's face. He twisted and writhed, struggling to breathe, so thick was the air with tiny fluttering wings. Through the chaos, he saw Pip rolling into a ball and Crumb stumbling over a potted plant.

Caw heard an almighty *crash* and felt a shower of sharp rain across his back. *Glass. Silk is just a distraction!* He threw himself aside as the bison crashed through the doors, followed by its mistress, and stomped to a halt in the bank lobby, steam rising from its back and nostrils.

In the next moment the moths lifted away. Light and air rushed over Caw, and he heard a terrified wail.

The bison was looming over Pip, pawing at the ground with its horns lowered. The mouse feral was pressed up against a counter, shaking in fear.

Caw's crows massed by the door, but he held out a hand to stay them. One wrong move and the creature could crush Pip or rip him to pieces with its horns.

"Smart decision," said Lugmann. He stalked past Caw, wielding his sledgehammer once more. His panther flashed its teeth in Caw's direction. Caw flinched as he felt the heat of the big cat's breath.

"No one do anything stupid," said the convict. "Tyra's beast can kill that kid in a heartbeat. It'll take more than a flock of birds to stop it."

Mr. Pickwick finally let go of the useless phone. He laid it gently in its cradle. "What happens now?"

"Show Mr. Silk to the vault," said Lugmann.

Mr. Pickwick hesitated, and the convict rolled his eyes. Instantly the panther pounced, landing on the counter beside the sparrow feral. It swiped a paw, almost playfully, across his arm. Pickwick cried out as its claws gouged through his suit and blood spattered on the floor.

"Do as he says," said Crumb, his voice quaking. "Lugmann, if that boy gets hurt . . ."

"If you do as we say, he'll live," said Lugmann.

Mr. Pickwick led the moth feral to a door at the back of the bank and tapped in a code. Caw angrily watched Mr. Silk's cream-colored suit disappear with Pickwick. The last time he'd seen the moth feral, Mr. Silk had plunged into the Blackwater, the filthy river that flowed through the city. Caw had assumed that he'd drowned.

"You're pathetic," said Pip suddenly, his lips trembling.

"Shut your mouth," said Lugmann, brandishing the sledgehammer.

"I'm not scared," retorted Pip.

"Quiet!" said Crumb.

"No!" said Pip. "Even if he kills us, the other ferals will still stop him!"

Tyra laughed. "With birds and mice?" she said. The bison snorted, its massive flanks heaving.

Pip swallowed. "You're just a bunch of greedy crooks," he said. "We work together, and you only look out for yourselves."

"Pip!" said Crumb. "Please, stop!"

"Boy's got more guts than you, pigeon talker," said Lugmann.

Some of the bank employees who'd been hiding in the back came through the door, shouldering the weight of huge canvas sacks with notes spilling out of the top. They gazed at the bison and the panther in terrified astonishment.

"Load up the van!" said Lugmann impatiently, waving his sledgehammer.

The bank staff carried the sacks through the broken glass doors and down the bank steps and began to place them in the back of the van. They barely seemed to notice the hundreds of birds massed outside, and as soon as they had loaded the van, they ran off down the street. Mr. Silk reappeared, and Lugmann tossed him the van keys. "We'll be out in a minute. I haven't quite finished here," Lugmann sneered.

Tyra summoned the bison to her and patted its matted fur.

"We've got what we came for, my friend," said Mr. Silk, a hand on Lugmann's arm. "Almost three million, by my estimate."

Lugmann shook off the hand, and his cold eyes fell on Pip. "Yes, but my pet hasn't eaten yet."

Caw tensed, ready to jump up. He could sense his crows outside spreading their wings. Nothing would happen to Pip, not while Caw was still breathing. . . .

Mr. Silk paused, removing his hat. He shot a look at Pip, who had begun to cry as the panther paced toward him. "Those weren't our orders," he said quietly.

Lugmann and the moth feral eyeballed each other. Caw hesitated, his breath catching painfully. *Orders? Who's giving them orders?*

"I'm . . . reading between the lines," said Lugmann. "Wait in the van, Silk. Unless you want to watch."

The moth feral replaced his hat, and without a backward glance, he swept out of the bank.

"You promised not to hurt Pip," said Crumb.

"No," said Lugmann. "I promised he'd live. He can live with one leg, can't he?"

"You've got your money," Caw growled. "Just go."

"Do it," Tyra said, eyes gleaming.

The panther opened its yellowed jaws wide.

2

Caw summoned his crows, driving them with all his willpower. As his birds shot into the air, he heard growling, and a pack of wolves streaked past him. Caw's heart soared. *Racklen must be here!*

Two wolves leaped onto the snarling panther, raking it with their claws. Another sent Lugmann sprawling to the floor. The bison backed off in panic, as three more snapped and growled in its face.

No, not wolves. They were too small and lithe. Their fur was sandy and pale, not gray.

Coyotes.

The panther rolled, then lashed out with a paw, as it backed away across the stone floor.

Tyra ran to Lugmann, but instead of helping him up, she grabbed the sledgehammer. She could barely lift it, and the crows swooped in, pecking at her wrist. She screamed and dropped the hammer, the head crunching into the floor. The crows' claws snatched at her clothes, lifting her up and dropping her behind a teller's counter with a thump. Pigeons joined the coyotes, and the massive bison bucked and crashed into furniture in an effort to escape.

Mr. Pickwick scrambled out of the way. Crumb swept Pip up in his arms as the panther spun and growled. It hurled a coyote across the bank as if it weighed nothing and swatted another to the floor with a howl. But more wild dogs rushed in, so many that Caw lost count.

The bison staggered behind the counter, emerging a moment later with a barely conscious Tyra, her collar clutched in its mouth. It dragged her out the door and down the steps, stumbling as fast as it could.

Lugmann was on his feet again, and with his panther shielding him from snarling coyotes, he ran out of the bank's shattered front door. They scrambled into the back of the van and the doors closed.

Caw rushed to the top of the steps, calling his crows to action. They swarmed the windshield as Mr. Silk cranked the van into gear. It lurched forward, crashed into a lamppost, then veered across the wet street and smashed into a parked car, scattering glass across the road. The back doors swung open and several sacks spilled out. Lugmann hauled the doors closed, and with a screech of rubber, the van tore off down the street, crows streaking from its windshield. Feathers and rolls of cash littered the ground.

Mr. Pickwick appeared at Caw's side clutching his bleeding

arm, misery etched on his face. The bank was wrecked. Blood spattered the floor, mixed with clumps of fur and feathers. Chairs were smashed, and a clock hung askew on the wall. Coyotes, around a dozen of them, lay down and began to lick their wounds.

"Where did they come from?" asked Caw.

Crumb was still holding Pip, breathing heavily. He glanced around as a new voice spoke up.

"Well, I thought you might need a hand."

Caw turned to see a man of about thirty skipping up the steps of the bank. He wore blue jeans and a pristine white T-shirt, with leather shoes and a leather jacket. His blond hair curled as it reached the nape of his neck, and his eyes sparkled a pale blue. He smiled warmly, and the nearest bloodied coyote pushed its head against his leg.

"Brave work, Vic," he said. "All of you."

The coyotes let out a collective noise, halfway between a purr and a growl.

"Fivetails!" said Crumb.

"Who?" said Pip, clearly as bewildered as Caw.

"Johnny Fivetails," said the man, holding out a hand to the mouse feral.

Pip looked at it, blinking.

The man grinned, then clapped him on the shoulder instead.

"Still in shock, I guess. It *was* a hell of a fight."

"What are you doing here?" said Crumb. "How did you—"

Sirens wailing in the distance cut him off.

"I'll explain later," said Johnny Fivetails. "Right now, we need to leave."

Still reeling, Caw led the way back to his house through the back streets. The rain was falling hard, and he and Pip sheltered under the umbrella while Crumb and the coyote feral followed behind. Crows and pigeons silently alighted on the buildings and the trees at regular intervals. If there were any coyotes below, they were well hidden. Caw glanced back and saw Johnny looking about and smiling, despite the rain.

"This place hasn't changed much in eight years, has it?" he said.

"Not really," said Crumb. He looked a little confused. "I thought you'd left Blackstone for good."

"So did I," said Johnny.

Caw muttered to Pip, "So do you know him?"

Pip shook his head. "I've heard of him, though. The great Johnny Fivetails! Fought for us in the Dark Summer. No one's seen him for ages."

Johnny must have overheard. "Never liked staying in one place," he said. "Always been like that."

"So why *are* you back?" asked Crumb.

Johnny grinned, revealing dazzling white teeth, and pointed at Caw. "Because of this guy."

"Me?" said Caw.

"Your fame travels, kid," said Johnny. "I can't believe I finally get to meet the crow talker who went to the Land of the Dead and returned! The hero who defeated the Mother of Flies! Hope you don't mind me saying, but you don't really look like a tough guy. Mind you, neither did your mom."

The sudden mention of his mother caught Caw off guard. "You—you knew her?"

"Sure!" said Johnny. "Bravest woman I ever met. Beautiful too, but I was only twenty at the time." He blushed. "Sorry—you probably don't need to hear that about your mom."

"It's okay," said Caw awkwardly. "Thank you, by the way—you saved us back at the bank."

"Lucky I showed up," said Johnny. "Never met a bison feral before, but we showed her who's boss, right?"

"Right!" said Pip.

Crumb looked less impressed. "So you were just passing by?"

"Not quite," said Johnny. "I've been in touch with Maddie. You know Maddie—the squirrel talker?"

"Madeleine," said Crumb with a brisk nod. "Yes, I know her."

Caw sensed the temperature dip, and he felt sorry for Crumb.

When Caw had been helping the pigeon feral shift his meager belongings from his old hideout back to Caw's place, a photo had fallen out. It showed teenage Madeleine and Crumb on a fairground ride, arms around each other.

"Well," Johnny carried on, clearly unaware, "she told me that there were some new ferals who don't play by the rules. I heard something about a casino last night, and a bank raid today. I guessed it might be Pickwick's place. Pretty fortunate, really."

Crumb nodded. He looked a little shaken.

"Maddie—sorry, *Madeleine*," continued Johnny. "She's looking great. Finally out of that wheelchair—I'm so happy for her."

Caw saw Crumb wince again. Time to change the subject.

"So are you staying in Blackstone?" he asked.

"I haven't decided yet," said Johnny. "I'm not great with decisions, to be honest. Hey, is it true you can actually, y'know, turn into a crow?"

Caw blushed.

"It's true!" said Pip.

"That's so awesome," said Johnny. "You have to show me that trick."

Caw hadn't even tried it since his battle with the Mother of Flies, but he sensed the power lurking within him. "Er . . . sure," he said.

"Where are you staying?" asked Crumb.

"Some dump by the river," Johnny replied. "The elevator doesn't work, and it smells bad, but at least it's out of this rain!" He smoothed strands of damp hair back from his face.

They'd reached a crossroads. One route headed west toward Caw's house, while another climbed toward the park in the north and the Strickhams' place. Caw wondered how Lydia was. She was the first human friend he'd ever had—and the best—but he hadn't seen her for over two weeks. He missed having her around, smiling and cracking jokes. Lately it felt as though there wasn't much to laugh about.

"Actually, I'll say good-bye here," said Johnny. "Need to find some food for the pack." He held out his hand to Caw. "An honor to meet you, crow talker. I'm sure we'll see each other around."

Caw felt a little weird but took it anyway.

Johnny shook firmly, staring at Caw. "You look so much like her, you know?"

Caw felt his cheeks reddening once more.

"Come to Caw's!" said Pip. "There's loads of room with us."

Johnny put up his hands. "Oh, no. I couldn't."

"I'm sure Johnny wouldn't want—" began Crumb.

"You must!" said Pip. "You just saved our lives."

"I guess that's up to Caw," said the coyote feral. "It's his place, after all."

Crumb had fallen silent, but Caw thought Pip had a good point. And perhaps Johnny could tell him a bit more about his mother too.

"You'd be welcome," he said.

Johnny shrugged. "That's very kind of you, Caw. Is it the place your folks used to have? I think I even remember the way." He pressed on ahead of them, whistling a happy tune.

As they walked back to the house, Caw thought about the bank heist. *A bison . . .* He hadn't noticed one of those on the roof when the Mother of Flies was creating her new army. He wondered what else had been up there—what other horrors awaited them.

And then he remembered something that Mr. Silk had said.

"*Those weren't our orders . . . ,*" Caw muttered.

"I've been wondering about that too," said Crumb quietly. "It sounds like they have a new boss."

"One of the other convicts?" asked Caw.

"Perhaps," said Crumb, but he didn't look convinced.

Caw shuddered as another possibility came to him. "You don't think the Mother of Flies . . ."

"No way," said Crumb quickly. "She's in the Blackstone asylum. Her connection with the flies is broken. She's no longer a threat."

Caw nodded. But somehow, he couldn't quite bring himself to believe it.

✦ ✦ ✦

The rain had let up by the time they reached the abandoned street where Caw lived. Johnny Fivetails walked by Caw's side, marveling at the dark, empty houses.

"This place has really gone downhill," he said. He turned to Caw. "Sorry, man. It's just a shock."

"It's okay," said Caw. "I like the privacy."

"The Dark Summer drove people out," said Crumb pointedly.

"I guess," said Johnny.

Caw suddenly felt embarrassed as they approached the overgrown front garden and boarded-up house. When Crumb and Pip had moved in a fortnight before, they'd been full of plans to give the place a fresh lick of paint and repair the windows. But fighting the escaped convicts had taken over from all of that.

Caw saw a faint light coming from the dining room window. The other ferals were already here.

He led the way to the front door and pushed it open.

Several people were seated around the dining room table, and candles were lit across the room. There were familiar faces—like Ali the bee feral, Racklen the wolf talker, and the bat feral, Chen— but strangers among them too. In the past couple of weeks, Mrs. Strickham, the fox feral, had been gathering to their cause all the loyal ferals she could find. Some had refused, but most had agreed to join them, reasoning that they were stronger in numbers. Across the floor lay an assortment of dogs, and a few birds and lizards clung to the furniture.

The room was heady with a potent mix of food smells. Some ferals were digging into takeout cartons while others had scavenged plates, bowls, and any container they could find from his kitchen.

When Caw had agreed that the good ferals could use his house as a base, he hadn't realized quite what Mrs. Strickham meant. But it was too late to go back on his word. It made sense to relocate here—their enemies might guess where they were, but at least no innocent people were living nearby. And Mrs. Strickham couldn't volunteer her own house. Caw knew that her husband, Lydia's father, would never allow the ferals to use his family home for their war councils. Until a couple of weeks ago, the warden of Blackstone Prison hadn't even known his wife was a feral, and from what Caw could gather, he wasn't all that happy about it. If it wasn't for him, Lydia might be here with them now. She would have found a way to make Caw feel better about all this.

The tall figure of Mrs. Strickham strode over to them. She was dressed in dark jeans and brown leather boots, with a pale roll-neck sweater. Her long hair was tied back. "We heard what happened," she said. "I'm glad you're all okay."

"They got away with the money," said Caw, lowering his eyes.

Mrs. Strickham touched his shoulder, and he looked up. "But everyone's all right?" she asked.

"I think so," said Caw. "It could have been a lot worse. . . ."

Mrs. Strickham's eyes shifted away, then went wide. A smile slowly lit up her face. "Johnny?" she said.

"Vel!" cried Johnny Fivetails.

Mrs. Strickham flew past Caw and embraced the coyote feral. Caw had never seen her look so happy. There was a commotion as several others crowded around, taking turns to hug Johnny or shake his hand. Even Racklen, who rarely smiled, was beaming.

Caw noticed Crumb was hanging back in the doorway. He didn't like crowds either. All these people sitting on his furniture made Caw feel like a stranger in his own home. It was becoming hard to breathe in here.

"So, what happened?" asked Mrs. Strickham, addressing Caw.

He felt the room turn its attention on him. "Lugmann hit Pickwick's bank," he said unsteadily. "We tried to stop them, but they had the bison feral."

"And Mr. Silk," Johnny pitched in. "It was well planned."

Mrs. Strickham nodded grimly. "I suspected the moth feral wasn't gone for good."

"Mr. Fivetails came to our rescue!" said Pip. "The bison was going to maul me!"

Johnny shrugged modestly. "Thank the coyotes, not me," he said.

"Our enemies are getting bolder," said Crumb. "A bison in the city—it wouldn't even have happened in the Dark Summer." He lowered his voice. "We think there might be a new boss."

Velma Strickham's eyes widened again, and she gestured to the wolf feral. "Racklen, Crumb, Johnny—we need to discuss this properly. Caw—do you want to get some food and join us?"

The room filled with a hubbub as the other ferals began talking with one another and with their animals. A snake wound down the banister and butterflies fluttered around the lampshade. A Great Dane lay sprawled across the sofa, drooling on the carpet. Caw was beginning to feel dizzy.

"I might go outside and get some fresh air first," he said.

Johnny looked a little surprised. "We could do with your input, Caw," he said.

A bright parrot flew past Caw's face and sparks flashed across his vision.

"Back in a minute," muttered Caw as his feet carried him toward the back door. He just needed to get away from all the noise. Crumb would say it better than he could anyway. He tripped over a snoozing fox, which bared its teeth at him.

"Stop it, Morag," said Mrs. Strickham. "Sorry, Caw, she's old and grumpy."

Caw stumbled into the kitchen, where a couple of lizards eyed him from the counter. Pip caught his arm.

"Hey, Caw, let me show you something," he said. "I've been practicing my power."

"That's great," said Caw as the room spun around him. "But can it wait?"

Pip lowered his eyes. "I guess so."

"Maybe later?" said Caw, feeling guilty as he grasped for the door handle. "I want to see, I promise."

"Okay," said Pip.

Caw flung open the back door and gulped in the cool garden air with relief. All those ferals inside needed somewhere to meet, but Caw felt a flash of annoyance at how they had made themselves at home. It was still *his* house, after all. He wondered if the arrangement was going to be permanent.

You okay? asked Shimmer.

Caw saw her perched on the kitchen windowsill, talons clinging to the edge of a broken plant pot. "I think so," he said.

Glum and Screech are up in the nest, said the crow. *They got some egg fried rice. I told them to save you some, but you know Screech. . . .*

Caw made his way down the overgrown garden path. It must have been beautiful once—there were still flowers of every description growing among the weeds and the remains of a delicate wooden archway. Caw tried to remember playing here with his mom and dad, but his memory refused to give anything up. A rosebush had grown away from the trellis in a wild sprawl, and he had to pick his way past the thorny overhang.

At the back of the garden grew a tall chestnut tree covered in knots and whorls. On sunny days, its huge canopy cast the garden in an emerald glow, but now its leaves were slick and dark with raindrops. Caw wedged his foot on a scar in the bark, pushed upward, and leaped for a low-hanging branch. Water droplets scattered from the drooping leaves as he pulled himself up onto it. As Caw scrambled swiftly up the tree, the tension across his temples vanished. Soon he couldn't hear anything but the leaves rustling, the dense foliage lending everything a peaceful hush.

The nest at the top of the chestnut tree was almost invisible from the ground, and Caw liked it that way. With the help of a legion of crows, he'd moved his tree house, piece by piece, from Blackstone Park. He knew that he had a comfortable bed in the main house, but it brought him comfort to have his former home close at hand. He'd even slept out here once or twice, and he had a feeling he'd want to tonight.

As he climbed in, Screech looked up, rice scattering from his beak.

You want some? he said.

"I'm okay, thanks," Caw said.

Phew, said Screech, head disappearing into the carton again.

Glum opened one eye, peering out in the direction of the house.

Bit noisy in there, isn't it? he said.

"I'm sure it won't be forever," said Caw doubtfully. He lay down across the nest, hands behind his head, and stared up at the gently swaying leaves. The only sound was the steady *drip-drip* of rainwater off the leaves. It made him think of a book he'd been reading—with a bit of help from Crumb. There was a story in it about an angry god who made it rain until everyone in the world was drowned. Well, almost everyone. One man and his family had survived in a great big ship called an ark. Somehow he'd invited two of every animal on board.

Sounds a bit unlikely, Glum had said when Caw told him about it.

"Maybe he was a feral," Caw had suggested.

The nest was the perfect place for Caw to empty his thoughts. Sometimes, it wasn't hard to fool himself that he was back in the park, just Caw and his crows, before his world had changed completely. Back then he hadn't known that there were other ferals in Blackstone. He hadn't even known there were ferals at all. Life was hard, of course, but it was simple too. *Forage, stay out of sight, and sleep.* No Spinning Man, no Mother of Flies, no fighting against ferals who wanted to kill him. But no friends either, other than his crows, Screech and Glum. And his oldest companion, Milky, who was now gone forever to the Land of the Dead. *No Lydia. No Mrs. Strickham or Crumb or Pip.*

No Selina.

Guilty feelings surged through Caw's brain. Poor Selina, what was going on in *her* head? Was she dreaming or just drifting on a sea of emptiness?

Caw sat up, rocking the nest slightly. "We need to check on Selina," he said.

Again? asked Screech.

"There might be a change," said Caw firmly.

It's Glum's turn, said Screech.

I'll go, said Shimmer.

"Caw, are you up there?" called a familiar voice from below.

For a moment, Caw thought about not answering. He was fairly sure Mrs. Strickham couldn't see him, and she wouldn't be able to climb up. Nor would her foxes. One of her creatures must have seen him come up—Velma had spies everywhere.

"Caw?" she said again.

"Ladder's coming down," he called out. "Stand back."

He'd found the old rope ladder already attached to the tree, and with a bit of fixing up, it was perfect for guests. He unfastened it from the nearby branch and let it unroll.

The ladder tightened and swayed as it took Mrs. Strickham's weight, and a few seconds later her head broke through the foliage. She climbed a little unsteadily, and it was odd to see her so unsure of herself—the fox feral was normally completely in control. Caw

31

offered a hand to help her in. For an instant, he remembered the first time he'd met Lydia, and smiled. She'd invited herself in too.

Lydia's mother scrambled over the edge, then crouched in the tree house, regaining her composure. She'd never been up here before. "Well, this is . . . um . . . cozy," she said.

It's not built for two, Glum snapped.

Mrs. Strickham looked at the old crow askance. "I might not speak crow, but I'm guessing that was a grumble."

Glum turned his beak haughtily away.

"Don't worry," she said. "I'm not staying long."

As she glanced around the nest, Caw wondered what it was she wanted.

"So, you know Johnny?" he said at last.

Mrs. Strickham smiled and nodded. "Very well," she said. "He saved my life, on more than one occasion. I never thought he would come back." She shook her head in wonder. "Anyway, Caw, that's not what I came to speak with you about. I wanted to thank you for letting the other ferals use your home. A place where we can gather offers us security—a lot of those ferals inside are scared of becoming the next target."

"It's fine," said Caw, sort of meaning it. "But is this really the best place? There isn't even any electricity. Wouldn't they be better off somewhere . . . else?" He knew it sounded like an excuse, but

Velma didn't look annoyed. Instead, a wave of sadness passed over her face.

"I wish they could stay at mine," she said, "but things at home are . . . They're a little *difficult*. Lydia's father . . . Let's just say he's trying to get his head around some changes."

Caw tried to look sympathetic—things must be worse than he had imagined at the Strickhams'.

"Don't worry, though," said Mrs. Strickham, with forced brightness. "He and his prison guards are working with the police to track down the escaped convicts. We can win this battle if we all pull together. . . ."

"I know," said Caw.

"Which is why," continued Mrs. Strickham, "I wanted to speak with you about the Midnight Stone."

Caw resisted the urge to look up toward the whorl in the tree trunk a few feet above Mrs. Strickham's head. Hidden inside that whorl, wrapped in a cloth pouch, was the Midnight Stone. Caw had threaded it onto a piece of cord so he could wear it around his neck, but the tree seemed the safest place to keep it out of sight.

So that's what she's after, said Glum.

"What about it?" asked Caw.

"It's a great burden on your shoulders, Caw," said Mrs. Strickham. "If ever you want help, someone else to hold on to it, then—"

"No," said Caw quickly. The Midnight Stone had been guarded by his ancestors for hundreds of years—since the days of the greatest crow talker who ever lived, Black Corvus. Caw's famous ancestor had persuaded other ferals of his time to lend a portion of their powers to the Midnight Stone. This was in order to conserve their lines, in case they were killed without a feral heir. The Midnight Stone could absorb the abilities of any feral who touched its surface and bestow those powers on a normal human.

Caw's mother had kept the Midnight Stone safe from the Spinning Man and had been murdered protecting it. The Mother of Flies had used it to create a fearsome army, and Caw had almost died getting it back. *The Midnight Stone belongs to the crow line.*

"All I'm saying—" began Mrs. Strickham.

"I can look after it," said Caw firmly.

You tell her, said Shimmer.

Mrs. Strickham smiled. "I know you can, Caw," she said, touching his knee. Then she took a deep breath. "I should get back to the others." She reached out for the rope ladder and placed a foot on a rung. But once she had climbed down a couple of steps, she stopped.

"One more thing, Caw," she said.

"Yes?" said Caw.

"Can you talk to Lydia for me? She's having a tough time. With things at home."

Caw swallowed. He wanted to help his friend, but he wasn't sure how. He knew nothing about families or family problems. He hadn't even known his own parents.

"Just hearing from you would help," said Mrs. Strickham.

"Sure," said Caw.

"Thank you."

As the lush leaves swallowed Mrs. Strickham, Screech flapped onto Caw's arm. *What does she want with the stone?* Glum said.

"You heard," Caw replied. "She wants to look after it."

Or maybe she wants to use it, said the crow. *If there's going to be another war, she could use the stone to create her own feral army.*

Caw hadn't thought of that. "No one is going to use the stone," he said. "It's too risky."

You say that now—

"Glum, can you go and check on Selina, please?" Caw interrupted. He had had enough of the crow's chattering.

Me? said the crow. *Why me?*

It's your turn, old-timer, said Screech.

I don't mind going, said Shimmer.

"No, Glum goes," said Caw. "Please."

All right, said Glum. *But I'm telling you, there won't be any change.*

He spread his wings and dropped out of the nest, gliding gracefully between the leaves.

The other crows were silent, but Caw couldn't shake the niggling doubts from his mind. Could Screech be right about Mrs. Strickham? And if she wanted to use the Midnight Stone, why wouldn't she come straight out and say it?

Caw's neck prickled with an uncomfortable sensation of being watched. He scrambled up a branch until he could push the leaves aside and peer at the house. *His* house, even if it had been commandeered. There was a flock of parakeets on the gutters under the roof's edge. The upstairs windows were empty.

Then a flash of orange caught his eye, disappearing behind the chimney stack. He wasn't sure, but he thought it might have been a fox.

Caw waited a few seconds; then he let the leaves swing back to their natural resting place and climbed down to the nest below.

3

Caw tugged his companion through the streets, feet splashing in puddles. The hand in his was sweaty. Selina's black hair was plastered to her head and her skin was pale. Her wide eyes reflected silver specks of moonlight.

"Come on!" he said, gripping her hand tighter. "We have to run!"

His breath was like fire in his lungs as they skidded around a corner. He daren't look back—he could feel them following—a menacing presence that grew all the time. They ran beside a looming apartment block, then plunged through a side door into a deserted stairwell. Caw's legs burned as they charged up the steps, tripping and sliding. How far was it to the top? Caw glanced down as they flung themselves from one flight to the next and saw a black tide swamping the floors below. It rose fast, faster than they could climb. Selina was pulling on his hand like a dead weight, panting.

"Leave me," she said. "I can't go on."

"No!" said Caw. "Don't give up now!"

He tugged her after him.

They reached the door to the roof quicker than seemed possible and ran out into the open space. It was the roof of Cynthia Davenport's apartment. There was nowhere else to run.

"They're here!" said Selina, terror lacing her voice.

Caw glanced back and saw an army of spiders pouring through. The eight-legged creatures clambered over one another in a greedy rush, scurrying across the rooftop. Caw felt Selina's hand slip from his as he backed away. She stood perfectly still as the monstrous tide of spiders approached.

"Hurry!" said Caw.

She turned slowly to face him, her mouth open in shock as she clutched her stomach. Her hands parted and he saw a red mark spreading across Selina's shirt. He hadn't heard the gunshot, but it was all happening again just like before. The Mother of Flies had shot her own daughter. And there was nothing he could do but watch.

The spiders smashed into Selina, rising up her legs and turning them black. She didn't scream, but her knees gave way and she fell into the insects' fatal embrace. Yet more spiders swamped her body. Caw's feet were rooted to the spot as Selina was carried like a coffin on a thousand brittle spider legs across the roof.

All too late, he ran after her, arms stretched out desperately. The spiders had reached the roof's edge. Caw sprinted, but each step *became harder, as if the air was thickening into a swamp.*

Caw? said a voice from somewhere.

And Caw screamed as Selina's body slid over the precipice. . . .

Caw, wake up.

Caw sat bolt upright in the creaking nest. The leaves looked ash-colored in the dark, and he could only just make out the silhouette of a crow perched on the edge of the nest. Glum. "Selina . . . ," mumbled Caw.

Yes, said Glum. *Something's happened at the hospital.*

Caw tried to calm his breathing. "I dreamed of her."

You need to come and look, said Glum.

Is she better? said Screech, hopping up to a higher branch.

I don't know, said Glum. *Something's happened in her room— the window's boarded up.*

Caw leaped up. Was Selina in danger?

He quickly fastened the Crow's Beak under his coat, then swung out of the nest and dropped from branch to branch, leaping down to the grass. It was a clear, cold night. He glanced back to the house shrouded in darkness. Should he wake them? No. No need.

He ran toward the back fence, ignoring the slashing rose thorns, summoning all the crows he could find. Black shapes flickered against the moonlit sky. Caw held out his arms, waiting for the moment when their talons would fall on him and their wings would make him weightless.

They flew at high altitude, the glow of street lamps and headlights illuminating the city far below. Caw and his birds crossed the river and then passed the ramshackle ruin of the church where Caw had once lived with Crumb and Pip. In the distance, Caw could make out the solid outline of their destination.

Blackstone Hospital was a towering structure of purpose-built concrete blocks, sprawling around a maze of access roads. The visitor parking lot was practically empty, and a lone ambulance with spinning lights was parked next to an open set of double doors. Caw and his crows circled over the main entrance. A mad part of him thought about transforming into a crow and flying along the corridors. . . .

Follow me to the back, said Glum, turning his wings and descending in a shallow dive.

The crows swooped low over trees and then banked up around the far side of the building. Glum landed on a windowsill four stories up. Caw saw that one of the windowpanes was gone, and a wooden board had been nailed up in its place.

Are you sure this is her room? he asked.

It's hers, said Shimmer. *I've been here enough times. . . .*

The slatted blinds on the other side of the glass were closed.

We have to get inside, Caw said.

As they flew away from the window, something caught his eye—a sparkle below. At Caw's command, the crows deposited him softly on the grass. Hundreds of tiny glass shards were scattered on the ground directly beneath the boarded-up window. Caw ran toward the main entrance.

What are you doing? asked Screech, gliding above. *They won't let you in at this time of night.*

"Wait by the doors for my signal," Caw told her. "I might need a distraction."

The three birds landed on a bench beside the front doors as Caw marched into the well-lit foyer. A man with a bandage over his hand was falling asleep on a chair, and beside him an elderly woman sat knitting.

The man at the front desk looked up. "Can I help you?"

"I'm looking for a patient," said Caw. "I think she may have been moved."

"What's her name?" asked the receptionist.

"Selina Davenport," Caw replied, before adding, "She's my sister."

The receptionist held Caw's gaze, then picked up a phone. "Hi, Marie—I've got a kid in reception. Says he's related to the girl...." He paused. "Yes, the Davenport girl." He smiled unconvincingly at Caw as the person on the other end of the line spoke. "Sure. Of

41

course." He put down the phone. "If you wouldn't mind waiting a moment—someone will be with you." The smile looked faker by the second, and the back of Caw's neck itched.

"Is she all right?" he asked.

The receptionist gave him a sympathetic look. "Please, just wait here."

Something was wrong. Caw leaned as casually as he could on the counter and turned his head toward the closed doors.

"Now!" he mouthed, and summoned his crows with his mind.

They took off as one and the doors swished open.

The man with the bandaged hand jerked upright with a startled cry as the birds flew through the foyer. The receptionist leaped up from his seat as the birds descended on his desk, squawking wildly. "What the—! Get out of here!"

Shimmer landed on the edge of a mug and tipped coffee across the keyboard. The receptionist picked up a clipboard and began flailing it at the birds.

Caw walked quickly down the corridor to the stairwell. He knew the way from his previous visit. The crows would find their own way out. A few orderlies passed him on the steps, but no one seemed bothered by his presence. Caw exited on the fourth level, found Selina's room, and tried the handle. *Unlocked.* He stepped into the dark interior, his fingers fumbling for the switch.

As the light flickered on, his heart fell. The room was the

same—a bed and several pieces of monitoring equipment—but it was empty, the sheets neatly folded.

What if she hasn't made it? What if . . .

But that didn't explain the broken window. Caw crossed the room quickly.

A few jagged shards of glass remained in the frame. He glanced around the room. Something was missing from beside the door—there was an empty stand where the fire extinguisher had been. *Maybe it was used to smash the window.* He went over to the wardrobe. Hanging inside were Selina's clothes: black jeans, T-shirt, and leather jacket—all cleaned, presumably, after she had been admitted. Even her ankle-high boots were tucked neatly inside.

How could she have run without her clothes?

Caw's heart was beating fast. *Maybe she didn't run at all.*

He looked again at the window. Four stories up?

It wouldn't be long before the receptionist came looking for him. He went again to the window, trying to piece together what had happened. Someone had come into the room and used the fire extinguisher to smash the glass. They had taken Selina. But who could make a jump like that? Even with a ladder, carrying a grown girl was treacherous, almost impossible.

Impossible for a regular person, but for a feral . . .

Caw's throat felt tight as he spotted something under the blind. Three small insects, curled up in death.

Flies.

Caw scooped their bodies into his hand. *So small, so delicate.* But Caw had seen what havoc these insects could wreak.

Maybe Crumb was wrong about the Mother of Flies. What if her feral powers had somehow survived? What if Caw wasn't the only one visiting Selina. . . .

"What are you doing in here?" said a sharp voice. Caw dropped the flies and spun around. A stern-faced woman in a gray suit was standing in the doorway.

"I—I came to find my sister," said Caw. "What's happened to her?"

"Your sister?" said the woman, folding her arms. "We have no record of any siblings. Do you want to try another lie?"

Caw wondered if he should call his crows. "Sorry," he said. "She was a close friend."

"*Was?*" said the woman. "What do you mean *was?*"

"Er . . . that's not what I meant," said Caw, beginning to panic.

The woman grasped the door frame like she was intentionally blocking his exit. "The police will want to speak with you about her disappearance," she said.

Caw could outrun her, if he could only get past. "When did she go missing?" he asked.

"Yesterday morning," said the woman. Unexpectedly, her face

softened. "Look—whoever you are—I'm Dr. Heidenweiss, senior pediatric consultant on this ward. Your friend, she didn't just get up and walk. She was in a deep coma. The authorities are treating it as a kidnapping."

Caw's heart plunged. He was right.

"If you know anything . . . ," the doctor continued. Something buzzed, and she looked down at a small device strapped to her belt. Caw took his chance and lurched toward the door. "Hey, wait!" she said, grabbing at him, but he tore free and ran along the corridor. An orderly was slowly wheeling a stretcher toward him.

"Stop that boy!" cried the doctor.

The orderly spun the stretcher around to block the corridor, but Caw vaulted over the top and carried on sprinting.

He took the left passage, then a right, then a left again. He ran under signs he couldn't read, past wards and nurses' stations. He found a set of stairs leading down and took them two at a time, all the way to the ground floor. As he raced into the corridor, he spotted a security guard straightening, hand going to the Taser at his side. Caw skidded around a corner. He could hear a baby crying somewhere. There were no windows, and he didn't know if he was heading deeper into the hospital or toward a way out until he recognized a sign. A white running man on a green background with an arrow. *Exit.*

Caw heard the squeak and slap of footsteps close behind him. He thumped through a set of double doors and saw another door with a bar across it straight ahead.

Please, don't be locked.

With his breath tearing through him, he slammed into the bar and the door swung open into the cold night air.

Come! his mind screamed.

And he felt his crows flock toward him as he ran. Moments later, they lifted him off the ground, filling the night with their raucous cries.

Despite the lateness of the hour, there were lights on in the Strickham house as Caw touched down on the lawn.

I'll say it again, said Glum. *I don't know what you're hoping to achieve.*

Caw ignored him. He'd seen what keeping secrets from his friends did. This time he was going to be open from the start. The hard part would be getting Mrs. Strickham to care. She didn't know Selina like Caw did. To some of their allies, Selina would always be nothing more than the fly talker's daughter—the enemy of peaceful ferals. But if the Mother of Flies was back, then everyone needed to know.

Caw was about to knock on the door when he heard hushed, angry voices.

". . . in the middle of the night, with no explanation," said Mr. Strickham. "Not even a phone call to let me know . . ."

"Time ran away, Tony," replied Lydia's mother. "I thought we'd discussed this before. You know I have to be on call."

"We're supposed to be in this together!"

Caw drew back—he shouldn't be listening to this. He sat down on the step.

As the crows settled next to him, Caw began to worry about what had happened at the hospital. What if they had closed-circuit TV? He'd be caught on camera, his picture shared with the police. . . .

"You going to sit out there all night?"

Caw looked up and saw Lydia's pale freckled face, framed with long red hair, leaning out of her bedroom window.

Caw smiled. It was a relief to see her looking so *normal* after all the weirdness.

"Can I come up?" he said.

"Use the drainpipe," she replied.

Caw shimmied up the metal drainpipe until he was level with Lydia's windowsill. She moved aside so he could climb into her room, and the crows hopped in afterward.

"How did you know I was here?" he said, dusting off his knees.

"I was awake," said Lydia, glancing down at the carpet. Caw immediately guessed what had been keeping her from sleep. Her parents' voices were indistinct through the floor, but they were obviously still arguing. Now that Caw looked closer, he saw Lydia's eyes were red-rimmed, like she'd been crying.

"It's like this most nights," she said, flopping onto her bed. "They're both stressed out all the time. Dad's trying to track down the prisoners with the police, and Mom is always having secret meetings. He won't let her foxes come into the garden anymore—says it freaks him out. Dad says he can protect the family without them."

She paused, and Caw saw that her face was beginning to screw up.

Maybe you should give her a hug, said Screech.

I don't think that's necessary, muttered Glum.

"I just want them to stop," said Lydia. "Sometimes I wish we could go back to before, before Dad and I knew anything about it. They say it's better with the truth in the open, but I'm not so sure. . . ."

She had been speaking into her lap, in a rush, but now she looked up at Caw. He hesitated, and she turned away, wringing her hands.

Caw? said Shimmer. *She's upset. Comfort her.*

Caw shuffled forward. He began to reach out, but Lydia suddenly stood up, putting on a brighter expression. "Anyway, what's going on with you?"

Caw dropped his hands awkwardly.

"Er . . . quite a lot, actually."

"I've been watching TV," said Lydia. "The news is full of stuff about the crime wave. They're even saying it's the start of a new Dark Summer. I'm guessing the escaped bison downtown belonged to a feral?"

"Yes," said Caw. "I was there."

Lydia's eyes widened. "No way!"

"But that's not all," said Caw. "Lydia—I think the Mother of Flies is up to something."

Any trace of excitement drained from Lydia's face. "She can't be. We stopped her."

Caw shook his head. "I thought so too, but I've just been to the hospital. Selina has been kidnapped."

Lydia gasped as Caw explained about the broken window and the flies. "Who else could carry her out of the window from four stories up?" he said.

Lydia went wordlessly to her wardrobe and began tugging on jeans over her pajamas.

"Where are you going?" Caw asked.

"*We* are going to find out what's going on," said Lydia. She tied back her hair, then pulled on a baseball cap.

"We are?" said Caw.

His friend started lacing up her sneakers. "There's one way to

49

find out if the Mother of Flies has regained her powers," said Lydia. "We go visit her."

Caw shook his head. "We can't—she's locked in the Blackstone loony bin."

"Er . . . it's called a *psychiatric hospital*," said Lydia.

"Sorry," said Caw, blushing. "That's what Crumb called it."

"If she's still there, I think we'll find out what she's capable of pretty quickly," said Lydia.

Caw felt anxiety squeezing his heart. It had taken more than he knew he had to defeat the Mother of Flies the last time. And even then, the battle could easily have gone the other way. *If she was back to her full power . . .*

Lydia pulled on a jacket.

"I don't think your parents are going to like this plan," said Caw.

"Those two"—Lydia pointed to the floor—"probably won't even notice I'm gone."

Angry muffled voices filtered up through the carpet.

"We should at least tell Crumb," said Caw. "And there's a new guy—a coyote feral. . . ."

Lydia nodded at her alarm clock—it was just after midnight. "You're going to wake them up? We can hardly go in with an army," she said. "Look, Caw—you only need me."

She spoke firmly, but Caw could hear the faintest hint of a plea in her words. *She needs to get away from here,* he realized.

"You're right," he said.

"Great!" said Lydia breezily. A smile lit up her freckled face. "Let's go catch some flies!"

4

As Caw and Lydia climbed down the drainpipe, Caw caught a glimpse through the living room window of Mr. Strickham slumped on the sofa, staring vacantly ahead.

"Maybe we should talk to your mom?" Caw said as his feet hit the ground, but he already knew what the answer would be.

"Please don't, Caw. It'll just set them off again. Besides, this is just a fact-finding mission. It won't be dangerous."

Caw instinctively scoured the garden for any foxes, glad not to find any watching them. Maybe Velma Strickham really had banished her foxes from her home. Caw felt a bit guilty about keeping things from her. But he'd done plenty for Mrs. Strickham already, hadn't he? Letting her invite everyone into his house. She didn't need to know his every move.

"Let me get us a ride," said Caw. He looked toward the sky and clenched his fists, ready to call the crows.

"Don't," said Lydia, touching his arm. "If there are flies about, they might see us."

"Then how will we get there?" asked Caw. "The asylum is

right on the edge of Blackstone."

"The number 62 bus!" said Lydia. "It might be public, but it's under the radar."

I'm not traveling on a bus, said Shimmer. *It's undignified.*

"You three can meet us there," said Caw. "Just keep low and out of sight."

Ooh—a secret mission! said Screech, hopping along the top of the Strickhams' fence. *Exciting!*

You'd better be careful, said Glum. *They'll probably want to keep you there indefinitely.*

Very funny, said Screech.

"Will you quit it?" said Caw.

Lydia grinned. "Hey, it's good to see you guys again," she said.

Just saying—it's hard to fly in a straitjacket, added Glum.

Keep up, old-timer, said Screech.

Unsurprisingly, Caw and Lydia were the only people on the bus. The driver didn't even seem to notice them as they hopped on board. Caw found it strange to feel the soft rumble of an engine beneath him, and it reassured him to watch the crows keep pace outside. He'd only traveled by car or bus a handful of times in his life, and it was a relief to step off when they got to their stop. The doors snapped closed and the bus pulled away into the night. Caw watched its red taillights vanish over a hill.

They were right on the outskirts of Blackstone, where the city's residential suburbs gave way to scattered industrial buildings, factories, and farms. Caw had been here only once before, when he was much younger, exploring with his crows. The bus depot was half a mile up the road, according to Lydia, and there was no other traffic and no sidewalk.

The Blackstone Psychiatric Hospital sign was painted on a rotting wooden panel set just back from the road. The building itself looked more like a spooky old mansion than a hospital, perched on raised ground, its turrets and towers piercing the sky.

Looks homey, said Shimmer. *I like what they've done with the bars on the windows.*

"It's one of the oldest buildings in the city," said Lydia with a glimmer in her eye. "It was built in the early 1700s."

Caw nodded mutely. The psychiatric hospital wasn't all ancient, though. There were a couple of ugly extensions on either side—plain, windowless single-story bunkers sprawling across the grounds. Spotlights cast eerie pale arcs of light through the deep shadows. There was a mesh fence, about nine feet high, and beyond that a wall. Caw shivered. If you were a patient here, you were obviously a prisoner too.

There was a large front gate with a guardhouse next to it. Inside, Caw could see a man in uniform reading a magazine with his feet up.

"What now?" said Lydia. "I have a feeling visiting hours are over."

Caw looked sideways at his friend. "I have a better plan."

"Disable the fence?" asked Lydia, rubbing her hands together.

Caw shook his head. He'd already begun to summon the crows as soon as he stepped off the bus. Now they started to arrive, a wave of dark shapes flitting overhead, joining Screech, Glum, and Shimmer. Caw guessed they could sense the electric current humming through the fence, because they landed on the ground around Caw and Lydia. The guard looked up briefly, then went back to reading.

"Flies or not," Caw said, "it's the best way."

Lydia held out her arms. "Come on, then, give me a lift."

The crows landed across their shoulders and lifted Caw and Lydia off the ground. His friend was grinning madly. "I love this bit!" she said.

Caw directed his birds to swoop over the gates and the hospital itself. From above, they could see that the asylum was built around two central courtyards. *Too out in the open.* The crows carried them across the steeply pitched roof, and then he spotted something more promising. He steered them toward a flat section scattered with bulky chimney flues. The crows set them down lightly, then gathered on the rooftop. There were no security lights or cameras up here.

A light breeze gusted through his clothes as Caw picked his

way between the chimney stacks. The turrets were huge up close.

"I don't fancy squeezing down a chimney," whispered Lydia.

Caw stopped by a metal hatch in the rooftop, with a simple looped handle. It looked newer than the rest of the building, and a couple of modern air vents had been fixed beside it.

"Hopefully we won't have to," he said. He reached down and tugged on the loop. It opened a quarter of an inch but then snagged. Caw pulled harder, but it didn't budge.

"It's locked from the inside," he said.

"Oh well, good try," said Lydia. "I guess we go through the courtyard."

Caw peered down over the edge. There were more security spotlights mounted on the walls, but it looked like they were switched off.

"Shimmer, do a sweep for any guards," he said.

The crow took off, diving over the edge of the roof. As she approached ground level, several of the lights blinked on, casting the courtyard in silvery light. Caw heard an electronic hum and saw cameras rotating to focus on the empty space. Shimmer banked and flapped skyward again, rejoining them just as a guard wandered into the courtyard. Caw and Lydia ducked out of sight with their backs against the chimney flues. The crows were dark silhouettes, unmoving.

"I don't think that's an option, then," said Lydia.

Caw chewed his lip. There was no way they could break open the roof hatch without some serious metal-cutting equipment. And Lydia was right about the chimneys—they were too small, and so were the vents beside the hatch.

Too small for a human anyway . . .

Caw scrambled to his feet. He edged back to the vents. They were about a foot across.

"A crow could fit down there," he said.

"Good thinking!" said Lydia.

Caw turned to Screech, who looked away as if he was suddenly very interested in something in the distance.

"Screech," Caw said, "can I borrow you for a moment?"

The crow plodded over. *Why me?*

"You're the smallest," said Caw. "Glum wouldn't fit."

Yes, I would! said the old crow indignantly.

Shimmer sniggered. *Too many french fries. Hey—I'll do it!* She hopped excitedly from side to side.

But Screech shook his wings. *Go on, then. Bring me back in one piece, okay?*

"Of course," said Caw. He closed his eyes and concentrated on his mental image of Screech. He felt his spirit detach from his body as it searched for the young crow. For a moment he floated on nothingness; then the crow body drew him in with a sort of feral gravity.

57

As Caw felt his talons touch the ground, he opened his eyes and found himself perched among the other crows. Several regarded him with curiosity, as if they sensed a different aura about him. He saw his human body lying motionless beside Lydia, eyes rolled back in his head. He took a few steps, getting used to the new configuration of limbs. He opened his beak—*Screech's beak*—and squawked.

In truth, he'd chosen Screech because he was the easiest crow to control. Caw wasn't sure why—perhaps because he was the youngest or perhaps it was just because their connection was stronger—but Shimmer was definitely harder, and Glum almost impossible.

"Are you in there?" said Lydia, crouching to look into his eyes.

Caw bobbed his head up and down in answer.

"That's so cool," said Lydia.

Caw flexed his wings and hopped up to peer over the edge of the vent. Below lay a black abyss, even with his enhanced crow vision, curving downward.

Good luck, said Glum.

I'm coming with you, said Shimmer.

Her talons rattled on the steel alongside him. Caw stepped forward and felt his claws skid for purchase. He tumbled into darkness.

He flapped his wings in panic, but there wasn't any room to extend them as he fell. He heard Shimmer cry out and felt her body buffeting against his. They crashed down onto more metal. Shimmer landed beside him in a tangle as dust filled his beak.

You okay? Shimmer asked.

I think so, replied Caw. He turned in the gloom and saw a dim light to his left. He skittered down the shaft toward it. Three slats crossed the opening, but by flattening his wings, he popped through to the other side. Caw was in a narrow stairwell with bare walls of patchy plaster. He guessed it was there to give access to the roof, for repairs. Shimmer flapped through too, scattering a loose feather. She was covered in dust and cobwebs.

Up there, said Caw. At the top of the steps, a vertical ladder led to the underside of the metal hatch they'd seen on the rooftop. On this side, a simple rusty bolt was drawn across. He and Shimmer flew up. Caw twisted his head and took the bolt in his beak. He strained his neck and managed to shift it a fraction.

Help out, will you? he said.

Shimmer joined him, fastening her beak on the bolt as well. Together they succeeded in moving it across.

Lydia, it's open! Caw shouted, forgetting for a moment that he was talking in crow. But his friend must have heard the sound of the bolt shifting. The hatch swung open from above, and she grinned down. "Nice work, guys!"

Caw flew out onto the roof and landed next to his motionless human form. He concentrated hard on letting his aura split from

Screech's and wobbled slightly as he reassumed his normal body. Screech blinked, then pecked him on the ear lightly. *You've got me all dirty.*

"Sorry," said Caw. "And thank you."

Lydia started to climb down the ladder into the service stairwell. Caw followed her, instructing all the crows to stay on the roof apart from Glum, Screech, and Shimmer.

At the bottom they came to a plain metal door. Caw turned the handle slowly and opened it a crack. The corridor on the other side took him by surprise.

The exterior of the hospital might have looked ancient, but the inside was definitely brand-new. The corridor was painted pristine white, with glass doors set into the sides every ten paces or so, each with a number above. Caw pushed open the door, checking both ways, and saw a security camera high on the wall. It was scanning slowly across the corridor, then reached its limit and began to turn back toward them. He quickly closed the door.

"There's a camera," he said to Lydia. "We'll have to time it exactly right."

Caw waited a few seconds, then peered out again. The camera was facing away. He beckoned Lydia and they left the stairwell and crept along the corridor. As they reached the first door—number 34—he sucked in a breath. A skeletal man stood perfectly still behind it, dressed in a beige hospital gown, eyeing them with pale blue eyes. He didn't flinch, or blink, even when the crows came into view. Behind him was a simple room with a perfectly made bed. A table contained a tray with an empty, clean plate.

"This place gives me the creeps," said Lydia.

The next door revealed a similar room, but in this one the bed was occupied by a tiny figure curled under the sheets. The food on the bedside table was untouched.

"Poor people," said Caw. He glanced back and saw that the camera would soon be on them.

The final cell was dimly lit, but Caw could make out someone moving inside. There was no noise at all—he guessed the glass was soundproofed. He hurried past.

The corridor approached a T-junction and Caw pulled Lydia into it, just as the camera swung around to face them. Lydia ducked, tugging him down too. She pointed to a glass-walled office just beyond them with a bank of monitors inside. A woman in a guard's uniform was eating a sandwich in front of the screens, with her back to Caw and Lydia. On the wall beside her were several plastic cards hanging from pegs.

"We need to find Cynthia Davenport's room," said Caw.

"And I bet those are the key cards," said Lydia, pointing at the office.

Shimmer hopped onto his foot. *My turn,* she insisted.

It's too dangerous, said Screech. *That security guard will see you.*

I'm not going in there, sparrow-brain! she said. *I've got a better plan.* She took off, flying low through the corridor.

"Where's she gone?" whispered Lydia.

"I have no idea," said Caw.

Sparrow-brain? Screech muttered.

Not a compliment, lad, chortled Glum. *I once met a sparrow who was scared of rain.*

One of the monitors in the office began to blink, the footage becoming shaky. The female security guard reached up to the bottom of the screen. She turned a dial, but nothing happened. The image flickered again.

The guard stood up, unclipped a holster at her belt, and walked toward the door, speaking into a walkie-talkie on her lapel.

"I've got a camera fault in D Block," she said, then paused. "Nah—it's probably just these old electrics. Looking into it."

She left the office.

Good old Shimmer, Caw thought. "Back soon," he said to the others. He tiptoed quickly into the office.

The key cards were numbered, and Caw scanned the names labeled below each one as quickly as he could. His reading had come along a lot in the last few months, but he knew he wasn't as fast as Lydia would be. Then he spotted it—*Cynthia Davenport. Number 8.* He grabbed the key card off the peg. Hopefully the guard wouldn't notice it was missing when she returned. Then he spotted a cable leading from the back of the monitors to a plug socket. It gave him an idea.

He took a half-empty coffee mug and sloshed the contents over the plug. With a fizz and a pop, all the screens blacked out at once. *That should buy us a few more minutes.*

By the time he got back to Lydia, Shimmer had returned.

"Got it!" said Caw, showing them the card. "We need to find cell eight."

Expecting an alarm to sound at any moment, or another guard to cross their path, they hurried along the corridors, turning corners until Caw lost his bearings. The numbers were counting down, and soon they reached number twelve, then eleven, then ten. Caw slowed his steps. These cells were empty.

Number nine was vacant too.

Caw felt his neck prickling. He reached instinctively for the Crow's Beak under his jacket, and Lydia looked alarmed. "What are you going to do?"

"It's just for protection," he said. "If anything happens, run, okay?"

Lydia raised her eyebrows.

"I mean it," said Caw.

The cell marked *8* was dark inside, but he could make out a figure hunched at the end of the bed. If she had seen them, she didn't show it.

Caw lifted the key card toward the sensor, then paused, his heart racing. The last time they had fought, the Mother of Flies had created a swarm of her creatures, a solid giant of insect flesh. She had almost crushed him in a fist made of flies. If *this* was a trap, then opening the door in front of him might be the last thing he ever did.

Lydia pressed a switch beside the sensor. Inside room eight, the light blinked on.

The figure on the bed shielded her eyes, shuffling backward. Cynthia Davenport seemed to have aged ten years in the last two weeks. Her hair was gray and messy, her pasty skin covered in blotches. Her once cruel eyes gazed at her visitors with a vacant stare from hollow, dark sockets. It was hard to tell in her hunched posture, but Caw even thought she had shrunk a little. Dried white spittle lurked at the corners of her mouth, and her hospital tunic was covered in food stains. There was no sign of any flies.

Caw looked at Lydia, who stared back sadly.

The crow talker searched Cynthia Davenport's vacant eyes, looking for some hint of the Mother of Flies.

"What now?" said Lydia.

Caw breathed deeply. He had to find out what had happened to Selina.

"Stay back," he muttered to Lydia. Then he held the key card against the sensor. The red light flashed green and the door slid open.

The patient in room eight didn't move.

"Hello?" said Caw, his heart beating so hard he thought he could hear it. "Commissioner Davenport? It's me, Jack Carmichael."

The patient blinked once. *"Fly, fly away,"* she muttered in a weird singsong voice, her head jerking. *"Fly to the sky, for his webs reach high. Spiders can't fly, but their spirits don't die."*

Caw frowned. "We need to talk to you," he said.

Cynthia Davenport continued mumbling as if he hadn't spoken. *"I spy his eight legs dancing nigh. You can try, you can try. But a crow can't fly from his spider eye."*

Her lips barely moved—but the strange chant made Caw shudder. He had been wrong after all. There was no way this woman could have kidnapped her daughter.

He took a step closer, and she shrank away, pressing herself against the wall.

"Please, we won't hurt you," said Lydia, entering behind Caw. "We just want to know about Selina. She's gone missing. Have you seen her?"

Cynthia's head whipped around at the sound of her daughter's name. Her eyes gleamed manically. "Oh, yes, *she's* here," she said. *"She's* always here with me."

65

Caw's pulse quickened. He lifted the point of his sword. "What have you done with her?"

Cynthia reached out a hand in front of her, lightly pushing the point of the Crow's Beak aside. Her nails were filthy, but she moved her fingers up and down as if she was stroking something tenderly. "My girl is here," she said. "*My pretty girl. Come to Mommy, darling. Let's go to the old well and draw the water together. . . . Yes, we can pick flowers, sweetheart. All the flowers you want . . . No, no spiders there, petal. Just flowers and water so clear you can see the past and future in its depths.*"

Lydia touched Caw's shoulder. She shook her head.

Caw lowered the blade. And as Cynthia Davenport continued to stare at the empty space where she could see an imaginary girl, the tension left Caw's body. In its place, a dull sadness throbbed. He wasn't looking at an evil feral any longer, just a broken mother longing for the daughter she had lost.

Screech gave a sudden warning squawk. Caw spun around, expecting to see a guard. Then Lydia cried out in alarm as a hairy shape leaped through the air and hit Caw in the chest. He felt something sharp scratching his forearm. "Ow!"

Caw dropped the Crow's Beak, staggering in pain as a small, pale-furred monkey leaped off his arm. It bared its needlelike teeth, and Cynthia Davenport began to wail as the monkey hopped around the room. Three more appeared—their horrible shrieks filling the air.

The crows flapped wildly, but soon both Screech and Shimmer were held in monkey paws, trapped on the ground. Glum tried to stay airborne, but the remaining two primates knocked him down and held him to the floor.

Get off me, you stinking fur ball! said Screech.

Caw started toward the Crow's Beak, but backed away sharply as a panther stalked into view at the doorway, followed by the hulking form of Lugmann. A scrawny young woman with her hair in ratty strands stood behind him. The monkey that had scratched Caw leaped onto her shoulder, hissing. The panther snarled and Lydia pressed up against Caw, her face pale.

Last of all, Mr. Silk sauntered into room eight. The moth feral's lips twisted in a cold smile.

"What a pleasure to see y'all here," he said.

5

Caw took a deep breath as he fought to understand what was happening. Their enemies, *right here.* "It was a trap," he said quietly.

Mr. Silk tipped his hat. "A trap you fell for—hook, line, and sinker."

Caw glanced at Cynthia Davenport, expecting her to drop the act. But there was no triumphant smile. She looked bewildered. Afraid, even.

Whatever was going on, the Mother of Flies wasn't part of it.

Caw closed his eyes and tried to summon more crows. If they could get through the hatch on the roof . . .

"Don't bother," said Mr. Silk. "We locked the door at the bottom of the stairwell. No one's coming to help you. We dealt with the guards too."

"But the flies at the hospital . . . ," said Lydia. The skinny, ratty-haired woman sniggered, revealing gappy, rotten teeth. She drew out a matchbox from her pocket. Pushing it open, she tipped half a dozen dead flies onto the floor.

Cynthia Davenport scrambled off the bed, falling to her knees. "My darlings! My creatures!" she cried, scooping up the dry husks in her palm. "Oh, my sweet children—what have they done to you?" Her eyes streamed with tears.

Caw didn't understand. Why would they bother planting dead flies in Selina's hospital room? And why hadn't Mr. Silk attacked him at Blackstone Hospital in the first place? There was no reason to bring them out here to the asylum. Was there?

Mr. Silk lifted his chin and looked down his nose at his former boss, cowering on the floor over her beloved flies. "What a pathetic sight," he said. "To think, I was once afraid of you."

With a twitch of his hand, moths burst from his cuff and flew at Cynthia's face. She squealed and flapped as moths drove her back until she was pressed against the wall beside Caw and Lydia. As quickly as they had appeared, the moths rustled back to Mr. Silk and vanished inside his cream jacket.

In the midst of Caw's whirling thoughts, a question crystallized. If it wasn't the Mother of Flies leading the convicts, who was it?

He glanced down at the Crow's Beak, which lay on the ground beside the bed. Lugmann or the panther would get to him before he could do much damage, but it might give Lydia time to escape.

"Before you do anything rash," said Mr. Silk, "we're here to deliver a message."

Caw glared at him.

"An old friend is back," said Mr. Silk. "He wants you to know that—"

"Enough of this," said Lugmann suddenly, shoving Mr. Silk out of the way. "I want my fun." He snatched up the Crow's Beak. "Gutted with his own blade," snarled the convict, his savage gaze fixed on Caw. "How fitting."

Caw's crows squawked desperately, but they couldn't help him.

"I'd hold back if I were you," said Mr. Silk. His head twitched toward the door, and then Caw heard it too. Something was coming. *Something rustling along the corridor.*

An unexpected look passed over Lugmann's face—of sheer terror. The monkey feral backed out of the door. Her creatures released the crows and sprang after her. "I told you to do what he said," she snapped. "Come on, let's go."

Lugmann tossed the blade on the bed and ran from the room, followed by the panther. Mr. Silk touched the brim of his hat. "Looks like he'll be delivering the message himself, after all," he said. "Good day."

He ambled backward from the room, then strode out of sight.

The rustling grew louder, sounding like a distant waterfall. Caw grabbed the Crow's Beak and stepped into the corridor with Lydia and his crows. Cynthia Davenport remained, crouched beside the dead flies. She looked up, her face racked with despair.

70

"He's here," she said, her voice hoarse. *"Run, children. Run!"*

Then Caw saw a great mass of black spill around the corner of the corridor, and it was like his nightmare come to life.

Spiders—thousands of them.

But how could it be him? thought Caw, backing away down the corridor.

"We killed the Spinning Man," Lydia whispered, echoing Caw's thoughts. "Didn't we?"

We have to get out of here, said Screech, hopping from talon to talon.

Caw was about to run when he realized he'd left the cell door open. He lunged back toward it.

Caw, no! said Shimmer.

"I can't let them get to her!" he said.

As he swiped the card back over the sensor, he got a final glance of Cynthia Davenport, cradling the dead flies in her hands. The door closed, just as the first spiders crashed against Caw's feet. He shook them off and ran after Lydia, the crows flying ahead.

As they rounded the corner, Caw saw a guard sprawled on the ground, his neck broken. *Lugmann's work.* Caw couldn't remember which way they'd come, but with the spiders on their heels, there was no going back. Lydia gasped as the arachnids swarmed across the floor, covering the guard's body.

At the next junction, the crows turned left.

This way, said Glum.

Caw followed, but then skidded to a halt as more spiders swept toward them from up ahead. He grabbed Lydia's arm and tugged her back in the opposite direction. The groups of spiders coalesced and scurried after them.

As they ran, Caw's mind throbbed with a question. *How can he be alive?*

Caw sensed they were heading deeper into the asylum. At any moment he expected to see the spider feral himself, like a monster from his nightmares. They turned several corners—left, right, right again—then more spiders blocked the way. Caw slowed his steps.

"He's toying with us," he said. The crows flapped, struggling to stay aloft in the confined space. Glum landed beside Caw. Sending them to attack would be pointless.

"Leave us," said Caw. "Get out."

No way, said Screech.

Two huge masses of spiders began to approach slowly from either side. Lydia clutched his arm. "Caw?" she said, as if willing him to do something.

Caw backed up to the wall and realized they were against a door—a wooden one, with a handle. Unable to believe their luck, he tried it. His hope flared as it opened.

Beyond it was a set of stairs leading down into darkness.

"Lydia! Down there—now!" Caw cried.

Lydia took the stairs, followed by the crows, then Caw slammed the door behind them. A horizontal line of light below the door filled up with spiders in seconds.

"Come on!" said Lydia. The air in here was colder, and musty like a cellar. Caw followed her, feeling his way with his fingertips along the rough stone wall.

At the bottom, it was pitch black, and he heard Lydia stumble.

All he could hear above them was the soft rustle of the spiders coming under the door and cascading down the steps.

I don't like this, said Shimmer.

"Can you see anything?" said Caw. Crows' eyes were much better than his own, especially at night.

Just a low corridor, said Screech. *Door at the end.*

Caw felt for Lydia's arm, and they shuffled along. He could sense the low ceiling just above their heads and moisture in the air. It felt as though they had been walking in darkness forever.

You're almost at the door, said Screech.

Caw sheathed the Crow's Beak, then reached out a hand, touching wooden panels studded with metal. The door creaked open.

Oh dear, said Glum.

"What?" said Caw.

Dead end. There's a light switch, on the wall to your left.

Caw felt for it, and suddenly was blinded. He blinked and

73

squinted; then his heart sank. They were in a room no bigger than six feet square, with peeling bare plaster over crumbling red brick. The light was coming from a single bare bulb hanging from the ceiling. But it was the picture on the wall that really drove fear through him. Someone had painted a mural in smeared black daubs. *A gigantic spider.*

They had made a terrible mistake.

The spiders were approaching along the corridor in waves, tripping over one another in their rush to reach Caw and Lydia.

"Caw, transform," said Lydia quietly. "Go and get help."

Caw could feel Lydia's arm trembling next to him. And he felt fear quickening into power in his gut. He could make himself a crow and fly to safety. But then what? He gripped her hand in his. "I'd never get back here in time," he said.

They pushed themselves up against the far wall as spiders filled the doorway. Caw followed their train right back along the corridor and up the stairs. He'd never seen so many before, except in the Land of the Dead. *Every spider in Blackstone is here,* he thought. *All coming for us.*

Then the creatures stopped, like troops forming up in perfect ranks—a solid line spanning the doorway as if afraid to cross the threshold.

"Why aren't they attacking?" said Lydia.

"I don't know," said Caw. He drew the Crow's Beak, holding it out in front of them.

The spiders began to move again, not forward but upward, climbing the door frame, clambering over one another. Others began to dangle off threads of silk from above. Caw could only watch as thousands of strands intersected across the door in a ghostly skein of complex webbing.

The spiders flooded across the strands, clinging to the silk and to one another, a solid mass of arachnid flesh. The surface flexed and bowed, and all the moisture left Caw's throat as he saw a shape materializing. Hollows for eyes, protuberances for ears and nose and lips, all supported by the web. Caw knew at once who he was looking at. A mouth opened among the mass of spiders, and a whispering voice emerged.

"*Hello, crow talker,*" said the Spinning Man.

Keeping one hand in Lydia's, Caw brandished the Crow's Beak.

"I killed you," said Caw.

The spiders rippled across the face, and soft laughter filled the tiny room. "*You cannot kill me, Caw, any more than you can kill an idea. My soul is undeniable. I have been watching you.*"

Caw's fingers tightened on the hilt of the sword.

"*How do you like this place?*" asked the man made of spiders.

Caw looked around the room. It wasn't like any other part

of the asylum. It looked old, and forgotten, like something from another time.

"*I wanted you to see it,*" hissed the voice.

"Why?" said Lydia.

The face lost definition for a second as spiders tumbled to the ground. It looked like at any moment the whole structure could collapse. But more spiders joined, and the features hardened once more.

"*Long ago,*" said the spider creature, "*a spider feral died in this room. It was a madhouse then, as it is now—not that she was mad.*"

"Then why was she brought here?" asked Lydia.

"*You'd better ask Jack that,*" said the voice.

"I don't know what you're talking about," said Caw.

"*But you will,*" said the Spinning Man. More of the spiders toppled off, and the whole face sagged an inch or two. "*Consider this the start of your education, crow talker. You will be going on a journey.*"

Caw kept the Crow's Beak raised. "A journey where?"

The spider creature sighed, and its lips turned down in a sneer. "*To the depths of despair and beyond,*" said the Spinning Man. "*I will take everything from you. Everything you hold dear.*"

Caw sensed Lydia stiffen.

"*Before you die, you will pay for the crimes of your ancestors with your happiness. The spiders will have their revenge and they will feast on crow flesh, even in the Land of the Dead."*

The words sounded like a prophecy, but despite the dread that prickled over Caw's skin, he pointed his blade at the creature's face.

"What have you done with Selina?" he said.

The figure's lips curled into a smile. *"Selina is mine now,"* he said.

The certainty of the words chilled Caw to the bone. "Where is she?" he shouted.

"She is just the beginning, crow talker."

Caw's rage boiled over. He thrust the Crow's Beak deep into the mass of spiders and began to rip the blade back and forth. Spiders scattered as the web disintegrated.

"Prepare yourself, Jack," said the voice, muffled. *"I am coming."*

With those words, all the spiders toppled into a shapeless mound. Caw watched with a sick feeling as they retreated like an ebbing tide, through the door, along the corridor, and up the stairs.

What was that all about? said Glum. *Why didn't he kill us?*

I thought he was dead, said Shimmer.

Caw's heart was beating so fast it was almost painful. He shook his head. "Maybe it was his . . . soul . . . or something. He said he wants me to suffer."

Before he kills you, added Screech helpfully.

"Let's get out of here," said Lydia.

Caw nodded, then glanced around the room. It looked like a

prison cell. Was the Spinning Man telling the truth about a spider feral dying here years ago? But what could that possibly have to do with him?

One thing was clear. He couldn't deal with this on his own. Caw sheathed the Crow's Beak and started striding back along the corridor. "We have to get back to the house and tell the others," he said.

He tried to sound determined, but he couldn't ignore the ball of fear sitting heavy in his gut. The Spinning Man could have killed him—*easily*—but had chosen not to.

And he had Selina.

Which meant she was running out of time.

6

"We need to get an ambulance out here," said Lydia. "And the police."

Caw and Lydia had hurried back through the psychiatric hospital and were now clambering out onto the roof. No one had tried to stop them—the guards and orderlies were left lying unconscious or worse, thanks to Mr. Silk and his friends.

All this just so the Spinning Man could deliver his message.

But how was that even possible? The white crows had torn the spider feral to pieces, back in the Land of the Dead. Caw had seen it with his own eyes. And yet that . . . creature, down below, was him. Caw was sure of it.

He summoned more crows and told them to take Lydia home at once. "Wake your mother," he said. "Tell her to come and meet me with the others."

"What are you going to do?" asked Lydia as the crows began to land on her outstretched arms.

"I don't know," Caw said. "I have to figure it out."

As he watched the birds carry his friend off into the black, starlit sky, he held out his arms, and his creatures lifted him from the hospital roof and began flying in the opposite direction. Soon they were crossing over the outskirts of the city.

There was something in the distance up ahead: a pale smudge of smoke, billowing into the night. Caw felt a twinge of unease rising in his chest. In response, the crows flew faster. The anxiety swelled into panic.

The smoke was coming from his neighborhood.

It was coming from his *house*.

As they shot overhead, Caw saw with relief that the house itself was fine. But the huge tree in the backyard wasn't. The branches were black and bare, the tips still glowing like burning embers.

"No . . . ," he cried.

Caw's tree house was a charred shell.

The nest! said Shimmer.

Johnny Fivetails was in the garden with Crumb and Pip at his side, half-empty buckets of water at their feet.

Caw jumped from his crows' talons onto the garden path. He barely broke his stride as he ran toward the pigeon feral, eyes glued to what had been his nest—his home for so many years. Leaves crisped to ash fluttered on the breeze.

"What happened?" he said.

Crumb looked at him with wide eyes. "Where were you?" he said.

"I was . . . seeing Lydia," said Caw.

"Thank goodness you're safe," said Johnny Fivetails. His face and arms were smeared with damp ash.

"The new eagle feral paid us a visit," said Crumb. "With a Molotov cocktail. I tried to get buckets up there using the pigeons, but I'm so sorry, Caw. It wasn't enough."

Look out below! squawked Shimmer.

They looked up to see sparks dancing as the remains of the nest shifted sideways, then tipped over. Caw shoved Crumb out of the way as the burnt timber plummeted, smashing into the ground in a shower of ash.

Something struck Caw's arm, and blinking through gritty smoke, he saw the cuff of his jacket was on fire. He beat at it with his other hand; then Pip sloshed water over the flames and they sizzled out. Caw winced as searing pain pulsed across his wrist.

"Let me see your arm," said Crumb, coming close.

Caw gingerly peeled up his ragged sleeve and saw the skin was red-raw and glistening. The pigeon feral hissed through his teeth. "Nasty," he said. "We need to get a bandage on that."

"I'll be all right," said Caw.

"Not if it gets infected, you won't," said Crumb.

Caw looked at the broken remains of his beloved nest.

"We can fix it up," said Johnny. "The important thing is that no one's badly hurt."

Caw nodded mutely. It had been his sanctuary, and now it was just blackened wood.

"We should go inside," said Crumb, touching Caw's shoulder.

"Just give me a minute," said Caw.

The others drifted inside. Caw waited until he was alone, then nodded to Screech. The crow knew what to do. He flew up into the dead branches, above where the nest used to be. A moment later, he called down, *Don't worry—it's fine.*

Screech flew back down to Caw, clutching the Midnight Stone by its cord. Incredibly, the stone was completely undamaged, protected by the whorl in the trunk. Caw looped it over his neck and resolutely turned his back on the smoking wreckage.

He tried to tell himself that this attack on his tree house was just a coincidence. That it had nothing to do with the Spinning Man and what they'd seen at the psychiatric hospital. Their enemies—Mr. Silk at least—knew where Caw's house was. They were bound to have attacked it at some point. But why destroy the nest instead of attacking the ferals in the house? It had no value. Not to anyone except Caw.

The words of the Spinning Man came back to him at once.

I will take everything you hold dear.

Caw had a bad feeling this was just the start.

✦ ✦ ✦

By the time Mrs. Strickham arrived with Lydia, Johnny Fivetails was fastening a gauze bandage over Caw's injured forearm.

"What happened?" said Lydia's mother. "It smells like there's been a fire."

"Caw, are you okay?" said Lydia, rushing toward him.

"Just a small burn," Caw said. "I'm fine now."

His arm still stung, but it faded into insignificance alongside the thoughts tumbling over in his head.

"We need to hit back," said Racklen. He and the other ferals were seated around the living room. It was four in the morning, but no one was sleeping. "Pip, have your mice heard anything else around the city?"

"We're not safe here," said a skinny man with a raccoon on his lap. Several other ferals began to chatter anxiously in agreement.

Caw glanced at Mrs. Strickham. She had dark circles under her eyes, and he wondered if she'd slept at all. From the taut line of her jaw and the furrows in her brow, Caw guessed Lydia had told her about the spiders at the psychiatric hospital. "It's the Spinning Man's doing," he said.

He spoke the words quietly, almost to himself, but they silenced everyone. Crumb put a hand on Caw's shoulder. "Listen, Caw, you've had a tough time, but—"

"He's back," interrupted Caw. "I—we"—he nodded to

Lydia—"met him tonight at Blackstone Psychiatric Hospital. Sort of."

The room erupted. Animals chirruped and screeched as their ferals began shouting in horror.

"I think you'd better explain things," Mrs. Strickham called out over the noise. "From the start."

Caw felt everyone in the room turn to him. He didn't know a lot of these people—they were newcomers, drawn out of hiding or back to Blackstone by the promise of safety in numbers. And here he was, telling them that the old threats were returning. He explained why he and Lydia had gone to see the Mother of Flies and the sorry state she was in. He tried to tell them about the face made of spiders and that the Spinning Man had kidnapped Selina but struggled to find the right words.

"Caw, are you really sure?" said Crumb. "Maybe . . . Well, it sounds scary as hell in there. Perhaps your mind was playing—"

"I saw it too," Lydia cut in. "It was him. The Spinning Man."

"So that's who Mr. Silk was talking about when he mentioned 'orders,'" said Pip in a quiet voice. "I knew he'd never let one of the convicts boss him around."

"But how is it even possible?" said Ali. The bee feral, normally dressed impeccably in a suit, had loosened his tie and unfastened his top button. His white shirt had smoke stains on it. "You told us you defeated him in the Land of the Dead."

Caw couldn't help but hear accusation in Ali's tone and saw that several others nodded in agreement. A woman with orange hair was stroking a lizard under the chin. "Yeah, that's what he said. But maybe it didn't happen quite like that," she said darkly.

"I did defeat him!" said Caw. "At least . . . I thought I did." They all stared, and he was forced to lower his eyes. "Look, I don't understand what's happening. But this is my fight. It's me he wants to punish."

"And we'll stand by you," said Pip.

"Ha!" said the raccoon feral. "You think he'll stop with you? We're all in danger, especially if he's got Mr. Silk and the convicts working for him. We should get away now while we still have the chance."

Johnny Fivetails stood up. "Not so fast," he said. "You're right, Pablo. We are in danger. But that's why we have to stand alongside Caw and fight."

Caw's spirits lifted a little.

"Fight the Spinning Man?" said the raccoon feral. "You're mad, Johnny. *You* might be a soldier, but I'm not. I just want to live in peace."

"I'm with Johnny," said Racklen. "We either fight as one, or we die as many."

"You sound like Caw's mother," said Chen, the bat feral, shaking his head. "Look what happened to her."

"Careful what you say about Lizzie Carmichael!" growled Johnny Fivetails. He marched over to the bat feral, bunching his fists. "She died so that others could live."

From beside the stairs a wolf leaped up, getting between Johnny and Chen and growling.

"Calm down," said Racklen. "Fighting each other won't help."

Johnny backed away, and the anger left his face quickly. Caw was glad that someone was sticking up for his mother.

"So, what do we do?" asked Ali. "They could attack at any moment—and next time it might be a whole flock of eagles with firebombs."

"We hit them first," said Mrs. Strickham with fire in her eyes. Lydia's mother had sent the Spinning Man to the Land of the Dead the first time—this was personal for her.

Racklen cracked his knuckles, then ran a hand through his wolf's fur. "I like the sound of that. But where? The asylum? The place will be crawling with cops."

Caw shook his head. "No, not there," he said. "I don't think what we saw was *him* exactly. Just his spiders."

"He used to operate from the sewing factory, didn't he?" said Johnny Fivetails.

Racklen nodded. "That area of the city is pretty much abandoned."

"Sounds like a long shot to me," said Mrs. Strickham. "He

knows that's the first place we'd look."

"Which means he'd see it as having the upper hand—he's waiting for us," Crumb added. "I can send some pigeons. Check it out."

"Good thinking," said Johnny.

Caw remembered the creepy sewing factory from his encounter with Mamba and Scuttle, the Spinning Man's henchmen. He didn't like the idea of going back there. But at least this time he'd have plenty of other ferals at his side.

"I can send out mice," said Pip. "Summon everyone who's not here."

Johnny Fivetails grinned. "Yeah, or I could do it the quick way." He pulled a phone out of his pocket. Caw noticed Pip blush.

"Even if we don't find the Spinning Man, we can hit back at the convicts," said Mrs. Strickham.

Everyone started to stand up.

"Wait a minute," said Caw. "What about Selina? If the Spinning Man has her, we've got to be careful she doesn't get hurt."

"This is the Mother of Flies' daughter, right?" said Johnny.

"Well, yes," said Caw, "but she's not like her mother."

"She tricked us before," said Racklen. "Led us into a trap at the zoo."

"That wasn't her fault," said Caw. "She's a good person. . . . She just got duped by her mom."

"If you say so," said Racklen coldly.

Johnny patted Caw on the back. "Of course she is, Caw. Right, everyone. Number one priority is to take out the Spinning Man. And if we see the girl, we snatch her. Got it?"

Most of the room nodded and murmured in agreement.

As the ferals began to disperse, Crumb came up to Caw. "You shouldn't have gone alone to the asylum," he said. "Why didn't you wake me?"

"I didn't think it would be that dangerous," said Caw, looking away. But the real reason was that he knew Crumb didn't care about Selina. He wouldn't have let Caw go.

"He didn't go alone," said Mrs. Strickham. She was standing right behind Caw. "He took my daughter and nearly got her killed as well."

"How were we supposed to know what would happen?" said Lydia. "Anyway, you and Dad were arguing, as usual. I didn't want to interrupt."

A pained expression washed over Mrs. Strickham's face. "We were arguing because he thinks ferals are putting you in danger," she said quietly. "And if you had been hurt, it would have proved his point. I want you to go home now, Lydia. You've done more than enough for one night."

"No," Lydia said quickly. "You think I'll be safer at home? They know where we live, Mom."

"She has a point," said Crumb.

Mrs. Strickham turned on him angrily. "Thank you for your parenting advice, Crumb."

"I'll keep an eye on her," said Racklen. "Once we get to the factory, Titus won't leave her side."

A lone wolf padded toward them. His head was almost as high as Lydia's shoulder.

Mrs. Strickham sighed. "But at the first sign of trouble . . ."

The wolf gave a rumbling growl.

Johnny Fivetails stood by the door. "We've got Chen's car and Velma's. Who else has a vehicle?"

Ali raised his hand.

"Me too," said a man with a weasel on his shoulder.

"I'll fly," said Caw. "My crows can take Lydia too."

Johnny Fivetails nodded, his face grave. "Okay," said the coyote feral. "We wait for the birds to confirm it's the sewing factory. Then we hit it at dawn."

7

"I never thought we'd come back here," said Lydia as she and Caw flew side by side in the predawn light. "It gives me the creeps."

Crumb had told Caw once that the industrial quarter of Blackstone used to be called the engine of the city, with shift workers streaming in twenty-four hours a day, long before the financial district was built. But Blackstone didn't make anything anymore. The old brick buildings had slowly fallen into disrepair. Most had broken windows and leaking roofs with crumbling chimneys. The cobbled streets that snaked between them were never cleaned, and were traversed by a lot more rats than humans.

Caw directed the crows toward the second floor of a half-built multistory parking lot a block from the sewing factory—the rendezvous. They flew in, landing on an empty stretch of concrete inside. Caw waved a hand and the crows took off again, all but Shimmer, Screech, and Glum.

"Do you think we'll find him?" said Lydia, hugging herself against the cold. Her voice echoed loudly in the abandoned parking lot. "The Spinning Man?"

Caw had been wondering the same thing as the crows carried them across the city. "Crumb's pigeons saw convicts inside the factory."

"I know," said Lydia. "But what about *him*?"

The screech of wheels made the crows flap their wings, but it was only Racklen's battered Jeep driving up from the level below, leading a convoy of other vehicles. As soon as the Jeep stopped, several pigeons landed on the hood.

"You sure the sewing factory is the place?" growled the wolf feral, jumping out.

"It's not empty, I can tell you that," said Crumb, getting down from the other side.

You want a second opinion? asked Screech. *Pigeons aren't all that reliable.*

"No, stay put," said Caw. It was a small reassurance, having his three crow companions with him.

Johnny started giving instructions as soon as he stepped out of Mrs. Strickham's car. He wanted two groups, one to enter at ground level, led by Mrs. Strickham and Racklen, and one to approach the upper-floor windows from the air.

"I'll lead the second," he said.

"I should lead," said Crumb. "Your coyotes will be on the ground."

"Thanks, Crumb," said Johnny. "But my animals won't be far away, trust me."

"But—" Crumb began.

"Leave it, Crumb," said Racklen. "Johnny knows what he's talking about."

Crumb flushed but didn't say anything else.

"What about me?" said Caw.

Johnny nodded. "You're my right-hand man. Plus, I don't know what this Selina girl looks like. You'll have to point her out to me."

"If she's even in there," said Crumb.

And if she's still— Glum began.

Shush! interrupted Shimmer. *Don't listen to him, Caw.*

"I never do," said Caw, trying to smile. But he knew there was a chance Glum's fears might prove well founded. When Selina had served her purpose, whatever that was, the Spinning Man wouldn't hesitate to kill her.

The sky was lightening to the east above the financial district. Johnny checked his watch. "Okay, everyone ready?"

As the assembled ferals nodded, a motorbike pulled up. Its leather-clad rider swung out of the seat and reached up to remove the helmet. Caw grinned when he saw Madeleine shake her raven hair free of the helmet, then open a compartment at the back of the bike. Half a dozen squirrels bounded out across the asphalt.

She picked out a crutch and limped toward them. As she approached, she opened her arm wide, smiling from ear to ear. Caw noticed Crumb beaming at her before she walked straight past him and hugged Johnny Fivetails, kissing him on both cheeks.

"Maddie! I didn't think you'd come," he said.

"You know me," she said. "I never did like a boring date."

Crumb cleared his throat. "Hi, Madeleine," he said with a shy wave.

She seemed to notice him for the first time, and her face was suddenly serious. She took both his hands in hers. "Hello, Samuel," she said. "Sorry I haven't been in touch."

He looked into her face and smiled. "I'm sorry too. I wanted to call . . . but I didn't know if you . . . " He looked her up and down. "I'm so glad you're walking again."

"It's been a long road," she said. "Lots of physical therapy. But hey—they doubted I'd ever be out of that wheelchair." She paused. "Seeing you and the other ferals again gave me a reason to keep trying."

"All right, we'll have time to catch up later," said Johnny. "Maddie—you're with Velma and the ground forces. Remember what we're here for—find the spider feral."

"Then what?" asked Ali.

"Then kill him," said Fivetails, his eyes cold.

Everyone nodded gravely, and Caw found himself doing the same. But Lydia was frowning. Maybe she was remembering the spider figure from the psychiatric hospital—how Caw had thrust his sword into its chest. Even if the Spinning Man was here, killing him might not be as straightforward as Johnny seemed to think. Would he even have a body to kill?

Caw was about to say something, but the group was already breaking up. Mrs. Strickham led her team down to ground level, pursued by a dozen foxes, along with Madeleine's squirrels, a host of dogs and raccoons, and several slithering lizards.

"Good luck," said Lydia before following her mother with Racklen's wolf.

"Be careful, Pip," said Crumb as the mouse feral jogged to keep up with the others.

"Let's do this," said Johnny. He climbed onto the railing at the edge of the parking lot and leaped across to the roof of the next building with easy athleticism. Caw jumped after him, sensing the rest of his crows swooping in from above, while Crumb used his pigeons to carry both him and Ali across the gap. Zeah, the feral with the parakeets, landed awkwardly as the birds struggled to set her down softly. "It's been a while," she said, stumbling.

Caw hadn't been a part of the Dark Summer, but he wondered if this was what it had felt like. An army of ferals creeping toward their enemies. Staying in a crouch, they moved swiftly across the rooftop. They paused at the far side of the roof, and Caw saw three coyotes slinking below. A buzzing overhead came from a swath of bees cutting through the air. Johnny held up a hand and silently pointed out the sewing factory. Caw's heart thumped in his chest.

The building looked even more ramshackle than last time. It was a double-story warehouse with a cellar floor below spanning the whole structure. There was barely a window intact on the second floor—some panes were just cracked, but others were missing entirely. Getting in wouldn't be a problem.

Johnny pointed to one of the windows and mimicked flying. Caw, Zeah, and Crumb summoned all the birds they could, and in a matter of seconds the rooftop ferals were being deposited safely inside.

Caw took a deep breath. They were in an old office, with leaning shelves and a desk littered with paperwork. A door led out into a corridor. Caw's heart skipped a beat as he spotted a figure watching them. But it was only a mannequin covered in pinned scraps of cloth.

He remembered the vast hall on the floor below, with hundreds of sewing machines neatly spaced on desks. But up here the rooms were partitioned as offices. There were several more mannequins in the office, and books of fabrics, and bulletin boards of clothing designs. Caw saw a dark oil painting of a bearded gentleman hanging lopsided on the wall. He wondered if the man had owned this place and what he'd think of it now. It looked like a hurricane had blown through. Caw stepped gingerly toward the door, and the floor creaked.

The air smelled slightly rotten, like animal droppings. There were leather sofas with blankets strewn across them. Ali held up a copy of the *Blackstone Herald*. "Yesterday's," he whispered.

As Caw passed through the doorway, he noticed claw marks on the frame. His crows lined the hallway.

Johnny clicked his fingers and pointed in different directions, indicating for them to fan out and investigate the top floor. The ferals split up and dispersed. Caw crept along the corridor, senses tingling. In a back room, he found a map of Blackstone pinned to a board, scribbled on with marker pen. He peered closer and saw that his house was circled. So was the psychiatric hospital and Lydia's place. There were other marks too—maybe some of the places the convicts had robbed or houses and workplaces of ferals. Caw shuddered. This was a criminal gang, well organized and ruthless.

"This is definitely the place," he muttered as Johnny appeared at his side.

Johnny's jaw clenched. "Hey, check out what I found."

Caw followed him out to the end of another corridor. There was an old elevator, with an articulated steel gate. "This will take us right down to the basement," said Johnny. "I bet they won't be expecting an attack from below."

"Won't they hear us coming?" said Caw.

"Not if we climb down the shaft," said Johnny. "You up for it?"

Caw looked through the gaps in the steel and saw a narrow shaft descending with thick cables in the center and pipework around the sides. A rusted service ladder was bolted to the wall.

"Okay," he said, with a tingle of excitement.

Johnny tugged back the gate. Zeah, Crumb, and Ali appeared at the other end of the corridor. "You guys take the main stairs," said Johnny.

Crumb frowned. "Are you sure about—"

A bloodcurdling yowl somewhere below set off a chorus of barking. Johnny clambered onto the ladder in the shaft. "Just go!" he said. "Good luck!"

Crumb, Ali, Zeah, and their animals set off at speed. Johnny was already clambering down the shaft as Caw lowered his feet onto the first rung of the ladder. Below he heard the sound of a gunshot, and a ricocheting bullet, then more animal cries. His crows flooded the shaft, hopping from pipe to pipe.

Caw and Johnny climbed fast. As they reached ground level, Caw saw chaos through the elevator gate. Ferals and their animals were locked in fierce battle with one another. A swarm of moths flashed past and landed on Madeleine's face, blocking her vision. She scratched at them as her squirrels leaped around in panic. Mr. Silk stood on a table, arms raised in orchestration, but he screamed as a squirrel scurried up his back and sank its teeth into his neck. A pack of foxes was gripping onto the flanks of a panther as it tried to throw them off. Lydia and Pip were sheltering behind one of Racklen's wolves, and Racklen himself was fist-fighting with Lugmann.

He managed to catch the convict's arm and hurled him across a bank of tables, smashing sewing machines onto the floor. Lugmann picked one up with a grunt and hurled it at the wolf feral, who ducked and then charged again. Monkeys clawed at biting squirrels, and an eagle swooped low over the room with a raccoon squealing in its talons.

"We've got to help them!" said Caw.

"No," said Johnny, quickly scanning the battle, then beginning to climb farther down the shaft. "The Spinning Man isn't there. We should keep heading down."

Ali had just burst through a side door, and angry bees swarmed into the room. Parakeets shot through the air in a riot of color. Caw spotted Mrs. Strickham staggering across the room. Her arm was bleeding as a vicious dog kept leaping at her. She caught it by the throat, falling to the ground. Then Caw saw a skinny convict with a metal bar approaching her. He had to do something. With a thrust of his hand, Caw sent a flock of crows squeezing through the elevator gate. As the man lifted the bar over Lydia's mother, crows raked at his face with beaks and talons, and he stumbled back, dropping his weapon.

"Caw, come on!" said Johnny from below.

Caw took a final glance, seeing Lydia break from cover and scurry between the tables. Racklen's wolf was busy swatting aside more dogs. Pip had vanished, but now pigeons had entered the fray as well. They'd already grabbed one of the convicts by the legs and were hoisting him up—he was gripping the edge of a table with both hands.

"Screech, Shimmer—watch Lydia," said Caw.

The two crows flew out onto the ground floor as Caw followed Johnny, keeping only a handful of his birds with him.

At last they reached the bottom of the elevator shaft and stepped out into a gloomy basement corridor. Caw paused, ears trying to pick out any sound. Johnny looked both ways. "Don't worry," he whispered. "My coyotes will be with us soon."

He reached under his leather jacket and withdrew a gun.

"What's that for?" asked Caw.

"What do you think?" said Johnny. "I'm not taking any chances against the spider feral."

Caw hadn't explored much of this area the last time he was here, but he remembered the vast warehouse room where Lydia had crossed over to the Land of the Dead. Was that where the Spinning Man had returned somehow?

It was silent, but Caw had the uneasy feeling he was being watched. Then, as they rounded a corner, he saw the cobwebs: hundreds of them strung across the hallway in thick swaths. A shudder ran down his spine.

"He's close," said Johnny Fivetails. Padding silently behind him came a pack of four coyotes. Caw felt a glimmer of relief at the sight of them.

"How did they get down here?" he asked.

Johnny grinned. "Coyotes are wily creatures," he said. "Let's check some of these rooms—call if you find anything." He darted off before Caw could respond. *Should we really be splitting up?* Caw wondered, but it was too late to argue.

Despite the mesh of webs, Caw couldn't see a single spider anywhere. He pushed his hand into the silky strands and tried to brush them aside. Webbing wrapped around his forearm, clinging tightly to his skin. He drew the Crow's Beak and slashed at the strands, cutting a way through. His crows had to hop across the floor to stop themselves from being smothered by falling webbing.

I don't like this, said Glum, sticking close to Caw. *What if it's a trap?*

"Then we'll find out soon enough," whispered Caw. But with every step he took, his heart told him to turn and run.

A flapping sound behind them told him Screech and Shimmer had arrived from upstairs.

"I told you to stay with Lydia," said Caw.

She's got a wolf, said Screech. *You need us more.*

We're winning that battle anyway, said Shimmer. *No sign of the Spinning Man, though.*

Caw's ears picked up a faint voice from his right. He moved closer and saw a door in the shadows.

"Help!" said someone from inside. "Who's out there? Please!"

The voice was muffled, but Caw knew at once who it was, and his heart leaped.

Selina!

"Be ready," he commanded his crows as he grasped the door handle. He tried to turn it, but the door was locked.

Give it a shove, said Screech.

"Please! Get me out of here!" cried Selina.

Caw slammed his boot into the lock and the door burst open. The room beyond was the same one he'd once been locked up with Crumb in—a repair workshop. There were broken sewing machines strewn across tables, lamps on workbenches, and racks of tools. Beyond that, he could see a figure crouching in a dark corner, face turned away. It was Selina, dressed in what looked like rags, her hair coated in something white. Caw thought it might be flour or sawdust.

She seemed afraid even to turn around. "Selina?" he said gently.

She was trembling. Caw couldn't bear to think of what might have happened to her since she had been taken from the hospital. If the Spinning Man had hurt her . . .

"It's okay," he said. "I'm here now. We're going to get you out."

"Where is he?" she said. "He won't let me leave."

"I don't know," said Caw. "But we can escape—if we go now."

He crossed the room and stooped down at her side. Selina pressed herself tighter into a ball, as though she was scared of him. Her clothes were the pajamas she'd been given in the hospital, torn and streaked with dirt. As he laid a hand on her shoulder, the trembling stopped and she froze. Selina's hair wasn't covered in anything after all, Caw realized—it looked like it had been dyed.

"Come on," he said. "It's me—your friend Caw."

The noise that came from her throat in reply was utterly unexpected. A laugh. Soft and low and utterly chilling—and not Selina's at all.

"*I know who you are,*" a voice said in an emotionless, creaking monotone. "*And I knew you would come.*"

Caw jerked to his feet.

She unfolded her body slowly, standing in a fluid movement that didn't look entirely human, with her arms held straight by her sides. Her hair was entirely white, and her face was just as pale. But her eyes were jet black, like polished pebbles. She'd only been in the hospital for a couple of weeks, but Selina's nails had grown several inches and were shaped into points, making her hands seem too long as they hung by her sides.

"Selina?" said Caw.

"*That name means nothing to this body anymore, Jack,*" said the cold voice. "*She is my vessel.*"

The voice was still a girl's—just—but the words belonged to someone else entirely. Caw's throat was bone dry as he tried to swallow.

"It's you," he said.

The figure didn't move, but her hair stirred and a long-legged spider crawled out. It scurried across her forehead and disappeared again. "What have you done to her?" said Caw.

"*I am the White Widow,*" said the voice.

More spiders appeared, pouring out from beneath the workbenches. They massed around Selina's feet in a perfect circle.

Caw lifted the Crow's Beak in desperation. "Let her go," he said.

A spider the size of a mouse dropped suddenly from the ceiling and sank its fangs into Caw's hand. He gasped in pain and dropped his sword.

"*I will let her go,*" said the White Widow, "*but by then she won't be much use to anyone.*"

Caw felt his legs unexpectedly wobble.

You okay? asked Screech.

Caw steadied himself against a bench. "*Don't worry,*" said the White Widow. "*The poison isn't deadly. I told you, didn't I, that I wouldn't kill you yet? Not until I have taken everything from you.*"

"I don't understand," said Caw, hearing his words slur.

"*There are many things you will learn,*" said the girl. She seemed to split into two as Caw's vision blurred.

"Caw, move!" yelled Johnny Fivetails.

Caw turned. The coyote feral was standing in the doorway, his gun leveled.

"No!" said Caw.

Johnny darted into the room, gun trained on Selina. She drifted smoothly across, keeping Caw between herself and the gun.

"Out of the way, Caw," said Johnny. Two coyotes stole in behind him.

Spiders flooded past Caw's ankles, and he staggered. He let his body fall, but his mind focused on one thought—his crows. A black shape knocked into Johnny's gun as the muzzle flashed and the sound of a shot rang through the room. Then another, as Johnny tried to shake the crows off. Bullets ricocheted off the walls and floor. "Caw, what are you doing?" he shouted.

"It's Selina," Caw tried to reply, but he wasn't sure if the words even came out.

The spiders surged past Caw and onto Johnny's legs. The coyote feral smashed Shimmer into a wall and struck Glum aside with the butt of the gun. Caw saw Selina backed into the corner of the room with nowhere to go. Then Johnny pushed past him, loading another magazine into his gun. Caw grabbed feebly at his leg, but it was no good. Johnny raised the barrel at Selina from point-blank range. She lifted her hands over her face.

With one last surge of energy, Caw lunged up into Johnny's

side, shoulder first. The coyote feral and Caw stumbled through the open doorway and sprawled on the ground, crushing hundreds of spiders as they fell.

"Kill her!" shouted Johnny.

Then Caw heard a terrible snarling and the crash of furniture overturning. He turned groggily and the room tipped on its head.

No, it wasn't the room. Selina—the White Widow—was on all fours, moving up the wall as one of the coyotes swiped at her with its paw. Another gunshot missed as she scurried upside down across the ceiling over their heads. Then she dropped onto the ground beside them and ran out of the door.

Johnny shoved Caw off him and scrambled into the corridor after her. Caw tried to crawl forward, but his limbs felt heavy and clumsy.

The coyote feral was firing wild shots into the webbing hanging from the ceiling, and more coyotes tore at it with their claws. Caw grabbed weakly at Johnny's ankles.

"Get off me, Caw!" said Johnny. "She's getting away." He dragged his leg free and ran to the elevator shaft. He fired three more shots directly upward. Selina must have fled that way.

"What *was* that thing?" asked a voice behind them.

Caw twisted his neck—close to passing out—and saw the other ferals spilling into the hallway. Mrs. Strickham led the way with her foxes. Crumb and Racklen came on either side. They looked exhausted, panting with the effort of the fight, clothes torn and disheveled.

Johnny let the gun hang at his side.

"*That* was the new spider feral," he said. "And thanks to our friend here, she escaped." He glared at Caw.

"She?" asked Madeleine.

Caw wanted to speak, but his head was spinning, and nausea made him want to retch. Crumb rushed down the hallway. "Police!" he said. "We need to get out of here."

"Everyone, back to the parking lot!" yelled Mrs. Strickham.

Caw wobbled to his feet, and Lydia rushed to his side. "Call your crows," she said.

They came at once, summoned wordlessly, shooting down the elevator shaft and along the corridor. Ferals scrambled in every direction as the sound of sirens, and then the pounding of boots came from above. Caw could barely walk, so he let his crows carry him up a stairway. They emerged from a side door into fresh air, rising fast into the sky. From above he saw police vans and spinning lights and armed cops encircling the building. Crows, pigeons, and parakeets carried Lydia and several ferals to safety.

As they landed in the parking lot beside their vehicles, the coyote feral came right up in Caw's face, shoving him back against a wall. One hand pressed against Caw's throat and he drew back his other in a fist.

"Get off him!" said Lydia.

Caw braced himself, but Racklen appeared out of nowhere and caught the coyote feral's arm before he could deliver the punch. The ferals, led by Mrs. Strickham, appeared in the parking lot. Many had cuts across their faces and limbs, and ripped clothing.

Johnny's face twisted, and Caw felt the hand on his neck tighten for a few seconds. He could sense Johnny's anger like static in the air. Then the coyote feral let go and backed off with a growl. A wolf moved to stand between him and Caw.

"What the hell were you doing?" shouted Johnny. "I had a clear shot. You could have gotten us *both* killed!"

Caw breathed heavily as another wave of sickness passed. At last he found his voice. "It was Selina," he said.

The news registered on Johnny's face, and his features smoothed as the anger seeped away. "*That* was your friend?" said Johnny. "The spider feral?"

"Caw, are you sure?" said Crumb.

Caw looked at each of their faces. He was glad to see, despite torn clothes and the odd cut, that all the ferals seemed unharmed.

"It was her," he said. "She'd changed. Her hair, her eyes"—he shuddered involuntarily—"but it was her."

"But she's the spider feral!" said Johnny. "That means she must be his child."

Caw shook his head. His mind was still a jumble, but he knew who he'd spoken to down there. "No, that's not quite right. It's the Spinning Man—he's inside her. Somehow. He called her the White Widow."

"How can she be the Spinning Man *and* the White Widow?" said Zeah, the parakeet feral.

"Exactly," said Racklen. "If she's the spider feral, she's not your friend anymore."

"And we just threw away the best chance we'll ever have of taking her out," added Johnny.

Several of Crumb's pigeons swooped down and landed on Mrs. Strickham's car roof. One let out a series of coos, and Crumb sighed. "The spider feral is gone," he said.

Johnny Fivetails slammed a fist onto the hood of a car three times, then turned and sank to his haunches against the wheel arch. He pushed a lock of hair back from his sweating forehead. "Nice work, Caw," he said.

8

Fifteen minutes later, the ferals were huddled deep in discussion, while crows and pigeons kept watch. Johnny Fivetails was pacing back and forth, casting a long shadow across the concrete. The distant rumble of traffic and blaring horns signaled the start of morning rush hour.

Caw sat apart, against the wall of the parking lot, inspecting the twin fang marks on his hand. The flesh was a little swollen, a purple patch of bruising spreading under the skin. Every so often his stomach would cramp.

He shivered again as he remembered the pale face of the White Widow, the hollow black eyes and voice filled with malice. Was that even Selina anymore, with so much of her life and spark snuffed out? Their friendship hadn't begun normally—with Selina wielding a baseball bat at Caw when he discovered her squatting in his house. And for a good while she had been lying to him, working for her mother. But when it mattered, when she had to make a choice, she'd stood up to her mother, and she'd been prepared to die to stop the convicts. Could the Selina he knew be gone forever? Or was her spirit still in there somewhere, waiting to be freed?

Caw's stomach spasmed again, sweeping all thoughts away. He clamped his eyes closed, waiting for it to pass. "Caw, we should get you to a hospital," said Lydia, placing a hand on his shoulder.

"No!" he said. "I'm all right."

"You don't know that," said Lydia. "The poison might be doing all sorts of damage inside."

Caw stood up shakily. "He said it wasn't fatal."

"And you trust him?"

"He wants to punish me. Selina's part of that. The nest too. But he's been true to his word so far."

Lydia sighed. "I know what that place meant to you, Caw. I'm sorry."

"I don't get it," Johnny Fivetails said, approaching Caw and Lydia with the other ferals. "If the White Widow's the new spider feral, she *must* be the daughter of the Spinning Man."

"Not necessarily," said Mrs. Strickham.

"What's that supposed to mean?" said Johnny. "There's only one way to become a feral—your parent passes on the power when they die. Well, maybe there's *one* other way. The way those prisoners got their powers bestowed by the Mother of Flies . . ."

Caw saw Mrs. Strickham flash a look in his direction. He

reached for the Midnight Stone as his eyes flickered downward. Yes—it was still there. He could tell what Johnny was thinking. If Selina *wasn't* the daughter of the Spinning Man, how could she have gotten the spider feral powers without Caw helping her? But there was no way her powers had come from the Midnight Stone—it had been under Caw's protection since that night on the apartment roof. And even if somehow Selina had touched it at the same time as a spider, that didn't explain how she had been infected by the spirit of the Spinning Man. Those black eyes had looked at Caw with real hatred. The White Widow wasn't just the new spider feral—she was carrying the soul of his bitter enemy.

When Caw looked up, he saw Johnny Fivetails leading the others farther away, behind some of the ferals' cars.

"What are they doing?" said Lydia.

"I don't know," Caw replied as Johnny flashed a glance back at them, "but I'm going to find out."

Maybe just stay out of it, said Screech, hopping at his side.

"No way," muttered Caw. Why were they sneaking off to talk in private? They were all supposed to be on the same side.

Let us listen in, said Shimmer.

But Caw needed to hear it directly. Staying behind the cars, he crept closer, still unsteady on his legs, with Lydia trailing behind him. The other ferals were talking in hushed voices, too absorbed in their conversation to notice his approach.

"And you trusted her—this Selina?" Johnny Fivetails was saying.

"She helped us," said Mrs. Strickham. "I really don't think she knew her mother was the fly feral."

"Or if she did, she was in denial," said Crumb.

Johnny put his hands on his hips. "And you think you can trust *him*?" he said, head nodding sharply toward where Caw had been a moment before.

Caw held his breath.

"Don't even go there," said Crumb. "You can't seriously be suggesting—"

"I'm ruling out nothing," said Johnny.

Mrs. Strickham held up a hand. "Johnny—I've been through so much with Caw. He's Lizzie Carmichael's son, for goodness' sake."

There was a pause, and then Johnny sighed. "I know," he said. "But his loyalties are torn. He attacked me when I could have killed the spider feral."

"If he thought it was his friend—" began Crumb.

"But you said yourself, he'd only known her a few days," said Johnny. "If that's even true . . ."

Crouched in the shadows, Caw couldn't believe they were talking about him like this. He bunched his hands into fists. Lydia laid a finger on her lips, and Caw nodded stiffly.

"We need a united front if we're going to meet this new threat," Johnny went on. "Caw's conflicted. He's upset. We should move the operation away from his house."

Crumb shook his head, but Racklen, Zeah, and Ali nodded. Johnny stared at Lydia's mother. "Vel?"

Mrs. Strickham closed her eyes in a slow blink. When she opened them, she nodded too. "Just let me talk to him."

Caw stepped out from behind the car. "If you have something to say," he said, "say it to my face."

"I know this is hard for you, Caw," said Mrs. Strickham. "Everyone's confused."

"So am I!" he said. "I didn't *attack* Johnny. I stopped him from shooting her. I don't know how to prove to you that I'm on your side, and I shouldn't have to." His voice was strained, too high.

"No one thinks you're not," said Crumb.

"I didn't say anything about you being a traitor," said Johnny. "But Caw—if you want to prove yourself . . ." He glanced briefly at Mrs. Strickham. "The Midnight Stone."

Velma Strickham's gaze was crystal clear, and in an instant Caw knew that she'd told the coyote feral all about the stone already.

Johnny shrugged. "I know what happened with the Mother of Flies—I know how she created her army." He stared at Caw. "You've got it, right?"

"Yes," said Caw after a brief pause.

"Well, let's use it!" said Johnny, stepping toward him. "We can create an army of our own."

"No," said Caw. "It's dangerous. The crow line swore to guard the stone."

Crumb squared up to Johnny. "You're talking about taking normal people and making them fight with us? That's crazy."

"Is it?" said Johnny. "Then what's the stone for? When a line dies, we bring it back. It's the ultimate weapon. Life after death, right?" His face was animated, his voice imploring.

"Slow down, Johnny," said Mrs. Strickham. "We haven't talked about this."

"Fine," said the coyote feral, suddenly calm. He took a deep breath. "Even if we decide not to use it right away, it's better Caw lets us look after it, surely? It'll be safest with someone who can guarantee its security."

"And someone you can trust?" added Caw bitterly.

No one spoke, but everyone was looking at Mrs. Strickham. She stared into the distance, jaw clenched. Then her gaze slid slowly to Caw. With a sinking heart, he knew exactly what she was going to say.

"We trust you, Caw. Of course we do. But . . . Johnny has a point." Caw began to shake his head, but she continued. "If the Spinning Man is back—if he wants some sort of revenge on you— then the stone will be better with us. Somewhere we can protect it." She held out her hand.

Caw moved back as Racklen began to approach with his wolf at his heels.

"Come on, Caw," said the wolf feral.

"Give him space," said Crumb. "This is Caw! He's one of us."

"Easy for you to say," said Ali angrily. "I lost half a swarm in there. They gave their lives for nothing."

"Stay back," said Caw. "You're not having it."

"Please," said Lydia desperately. "Leave him alone, all of you."

"Be honest, Caw," said Johnny. "Did you use the Midnight Stone on your pal Selina? Maybe you felt sorry for her. Maybe you thought giving her powers was the only way to save her."

"No," said Caw. "You've got it all wrong."

His back touched the low wall at the edge of the parking lot.

"Why are you running away?" asked Johnny.

"Leave him alone!" said Lydia again, lunging forward. Mrs. Strickham caught her daughter and held her back.

"Is it in your pocket?" asked Johnny.

"Just hand it over," added Racklen.

Caw, said Glum. *On your left.*

Two coyotes glided across the parking lot floor.

"There's no need for that," said Crumb. He put a hand on Johnny's shoulder, but the coyote feral pulled free.

"Get away from me!" Caw said. And before he had even thought about it properly, he'd drawn the Crow's Beak.

"Or what?" said Johnny, putting up both hands. "You'll stab me? You sure we're on the same side?"

"Caw, don't," said Pip. He looked close to tears.

"Calm down, everyone," said Mrs. Strickham. "Remember who we are! Caw, let's talk this out."

"You just want to take the stone," said Caw. "You've already made up your mind."

Johnny whipped out a hand and batted the Crow's Beak aside. Caw watched it skitter across the concrete, slide under the railings, and fall over the edge of the parking lot.

"Give me the Midnight Stone," said Johnny. "We'll look after it, I promise."

Racklen and Ali were coming at him from either side.

"Back off," said Caw as his mind screamed for him to fly. And then Johnny's face creased in confusion as Caw's skeleton seemed to soften and shrink. Caw's body dynamics turned upside down, his legs stiffening and strength flowing to his powerful shoulders.

"Hey, what are you— No!" shouted the coyote feral.

The world bent into curves as Caw became a crow.

The coyote feral lunged forward and in the same instant Shimmer and Screech flapped in his face. Johnny cried out, and Caw rolled over the top of the railings. He was falling for a second, before his wings caught the air and he swooped away. Looking back, he saw Lydia calling out to him. "Caw!" she yelled. "Come back!"

Let's get out of here, said Glum.

Caw hovered, waiting for Shimmer and Screech, then climbed with powerful wing strokes away from the parking lot.

We've got company, said Shimmer.

Pigeons were flocking over the edge of the building—hundreds of them.

Caw summoned his murder, and like a black swarm, more crows rose from the ground below. He needed to get away, but pigeons, as Crumb never tired of telling him, were faster than crows, and soon they were surrounded.

Split up and lose them, commanded Caw.

His crows burst across the sky. The pigeons scattered, each one tracking a different crow. Caw flew low between the buildings, zipping down an alley, under an old bridge, then climbing the other side. Pigeons were faster, but crows were more agile. He looped under the bridge a second time, then perched on one of the steel supports beneath. The pigeon chasing him shot past and flew on.

Caw waited, his crow heart thudding. It had happened so fast. They'd all turned on him.

Shimmer, Screech, and Glum glided in under the bridge and landed at his side.

That was crazy, said Shimmer.

We got away, though, said Screech. *What now?*

Caw thought for a moment. He'd left the Crow's Beak behind.

Perhaps he could go back. He could explain properly, say sorry for drawing his sword and— No! He didn't owe them an apology.

He couldn't go back to his house, and Lydia's place wasn't safe either, now that he couldn't rely on Mrs. Strickham.

Then it came to him. He knew only one person who could help now. The problem was, Caw didn't have the first clue where to find him.

Spreading his wings, he dropped back into the air and flew out from under the bridge. A small group of half a dozen crows were loitering on a rotting window box hanging off an abandoned tenement. He recognized one as Krak, a tough, no-nonsense female who was Shimmer's aunt—not that such family relationships meant much to crows. Caw landed beside the other crows, and they shuffled along.

I need you to go back for the Crow's Beak, he said. *But if it's too hard to retrieve, just leave it.*

Define hard, said Krak.

Caw smiled inside. *Just don't get hurt,* he said.

All the crows took off in a black stream except for Glum, Screech, and Shimmer.

And I need you to look for cats, he told Screech and Shimmer. *Spread the word—report to the old power plant, I'll be waiting there.*

Cats? said Screech. *Horrible creatures . . .*

Look for any hanging around in groups, said Caw. *Acting weirdly.*

What d'you want with them? asked Glum.

If we find cats, we can find Felix Quaker, replied Caw with a grimace. *Glum, you come with me.*

Felix Quaker might just be the only friend Caw had left.

The old power plant was a wasteland: a sprawl of corrugated steel and bare brick buildings surrounded by chain-link fencing. Huge rusting vats and ugly towers stood lifeless against the horizon. An offshoot of the Blackwater River that had once flowed under cooling towers came to rest here in stagnant murky pools. The gravel roads that years ago had been busy with trucks were now overgrown with weeds. One side of the plant had become a rubbish dump for old electrical appliances and metal waste—washing machines, TVs, and twisted girders.

No one ever came here now.

Still in crow form, Caw landed on the edge of an empty steel drum. Beside him, balancing on a lopsided aerial antenna, Glum shook out his feathers.

You really think the cat feral can help? he asked.

He's an expert on feral lore and our entire history, said Caw. *If there's a way to help Selina, he'll know it.*

It was sometime later when the rest of the crows began to arrive. Most had no information of any use, but Morton, an old warrior crow who'd lived through the Dark Summer, brought the news Caw had been hoping for.

There were three of them, he said. *Looking shifty. In the Lanes.*

Caw felt a surge of hope. The Lanes were all that remained of old Blackstone and lay beside what had once been the river docks. Most of the buildings there were cheap hostels, pawn shops, or discount stores. Caw had occasionally walked the streets there when he was younger. It was the one place in Blackstone that a boy on his own dressed in grubby, torn clothes attracted little attention.

It seemed an odd place for Quaker to be lurking—there were no restaurants, or tailors, or shops catering to the finer things in life that he enjoyed.

But if there were cats there, congregating . . .

Caw told his crows to stay where they were, apart from Morton and the three who always stuck by him. They flew off toward the river.

Glum pumped his wings to stay alongside Caw. *They're worried,* he said.

Who? said Caw.

The crows. They never liked Selina.

They don't know her like I do, said Caw.

Are you sure you do *know her?* asked Glum.

Caw didn't answer right away. He remembered how the last time he'd seen her she'd defied gravity, scurrying across the ceiling. He remembered the way she'd looked, with her bleached hair and eyes with no whites. If she was the White Widow, was there any of Selina left in her?

They're scared too, said Glum. *They fear the spiders will be too powerful this time.*

Give it a rest, said Screech. *We'll fight them like we always do. And if Caw says we rescue Selina, I say we help him.*

I never said I wouldn't, said Glum grumpily. *I'm just wondering if we're doing the right thing.*

What other options are there? asked Caw, his anger rising.

Glum was panting as he tried to keep up. *Only that you don't . . . have to do . . . this alone*, he said. *It's not your job to fix every problem.*

Caw put on a burst of speed to put some distance between them. Glum might be right, but the other ferals had hardly given him a choice, had they? They just wanted to kill the White Widow and forget all about Selina.

Finally, they reached the winding alleys that made up the Lanes. From above, the tall, mismatched buildings seemed to lean toward one another in huddles.

That's the place, said Morton, with a twitch of his beak toward a pitched roof with an open skylight. *The cats disappeared in there.*

Thank you, said Caw. *Return to the others. We'll be back soon.*

Caw swooped down and let his talons settle on the rooftop, where they became feet again at last. It was the longest time he'd ever spent as a crow. In human form once more, he peered through the skylight and saw a dim room inside. He placed his hand on the window frame, and a furry paw lashed up and raked him across the wrist. Caw drew it back with a gasp.

He heard rapid footsteps; then Felix Quaker appeared, clutching a cricket bat in one hand and a cutthroat razor in the other. "Who's that?" Quaker shouted.

He was wearing a scarlet dressing gown with satin trim, and half his doughy face was still covered in shaving foam. His wavy gray hair hung untidily over his shoulders. "Caw?" he said, eyes widening.

The cat hissed.

"Can I come in?" asked Caw.

Quaker rested the cricket bat on a table. "How did you find me?" he asked. "For pity's sake, Bluebeard. Let him past."

Caw cautiously opened the window wider, then lowered himself through, dropping onto worn, creaking floorboards. His three crows followed.

A dozen cats watched Caw suspiciously from the corners of the room.

"Welcome to my palace," said the cat feral joylessly.

Caw couldn't imagine anything more different from the splendor of Quaker's old residence, Gort House. In these cramped lodgings, there was just a single armchair with the stuffing bursting out, and a footstool. A camping stove with a small saucepan sat on a battered old desk. Only the shelves contained any vestige of Gort House, lined with ancient-looking objects that Caw guessed were feral artifacts—a feathered wand, an ornate glass cup, a skull that might have belonged to a large dog or maybe a pig or a goat. . . .

"Tea?" said Felix as a cat curled itself into the armchair and closed its eyes. "I'm afraid I have no fresh leaves. Only bags."

"No, thank you," said Caw. He looked around and saw a paltry row of leather-bound books—nothing like the vast library in Quaker's old house. "I need your help."

Quaker snorted and put a steel kettle on the stove's ring, lighting it with a match. "And what help can I possibly be to the crow talker?"

He sat on the footstool with a bowl of water and a cracked mirror in front of him, and recommenced shaving his chin with short, brisk strokes of the razor.

"The Spinning Man is back," said Caw.

Quaker paused, and his eyes met Caw's in the mirror. Then he continued shaving.

"That is not possible," he said quietly.

"He took Selina from the hospital—somehow," said Caw. "She calls herself the White Widow. He spoke to me—*through her.*"

Quaker wiped his face on a moth-eaten towel. It seemed like he had aged ten years in the last two weeks. He'd lost weight, and his legs looked skinny in his baggy trousers and shirt. His face sagged in fleshy folds.

"Well?" said Caw. "Don't you have anything to say?"

The kettle whistled, and Quaker shuffled over, dropping a teabag into a mug and pouring the steaming water.

"You're sure you don't want one?"

Ask him if he's got any cookies, said Screech.

"No!" said Caw. "Are you even listening?"

Quaker turned and hissed at the cat on the chair, which unfurled sleepily and hopped off. He sat down heavily. "I heard things were bad in the city," said Quaker.

"The convicts are getting more powerful with every day," said Caw. "And they're working for the White Widow now. We don't know what to do."

"You could run away," said Quaker. "If he's found a way back, then his powers are beyond your comprehension."

"That's why I came here," said Caw. "I need you."

Quaker nursed his tea in both hands. "I am not a fighter. You need Velma Strickham. Racklen. You need ferals who have fought him before."

"They want to *kill* Selina," said Caw.

"This 'White Widow,' you mean?" said Quaker. He looked at Caw with an arched brow and sipped his tea.

Caw shook his head angrily. "There must be another way. What about the Midnight Stone? It can suck out feral powers, can't it?"

Quaker looked up, his eyes flashing. "The Midnight Stone is dangerous," he said. "How would you ever get this new spider feral to touch it without putting it in her hands? If she—or, worse still, *he*—has it, that could be the end of us all."

Caw hated the tone of Quaker's voice. *Defeated.* Cowardly, though that was hardly a surprise. He wanted to smash the mug out of the cat feral's hands and haul him up by his collar. "I won't let them kill her."

"Ask yourself—is she better off dead?" said Quaker.

"Of course not!" said Caw.

Quaker sighed. "If the Spinning Man's spirit has possessed Selina—and I really have no idea *how* that could have happened—it is beyond me how to draw him out again."

"You were my last hope," said Caw.

A gray cat hopped up onto the desk, and Quaker absently stroked its head. "But . . . ," he said. "There might be another use for the stone. Do you have it with you now?

Caw reached under his collar and pulled it out, still safely wrapped in its pouch on the cord around his neck.

Quaker visibly stiffened, and though his eyes followed it, he didn't come any closer.

"It is said that your ancestor, Black Corvus, was the most powerful feral who ever lived," said Quaker. "Far more powerful than his contemporaries. Few people know this, but when he died, his daughter, the next crow feral, could barely summon the birds to her for many years. Some surmised that Black Corvus had invested his feral spirit *into* the Midnight Stone in his final hours. . . ."

"But how? And why?" said Caw.

Quaker shrugged. "Perhaps he couldn't bear the idea of dying and thought it was a way to live on. There are some who say he was jealous of anyone else having his power. Even his own flesh and blood."

Caw frowned. "But Black Corvus created the Midnight Stone for the good of all ferals, didn't he?" He had seen Black Corvus just once before, in the memories of Bootlace the worm feral—his ancestor had a fierce expression and a voice filled with confidence. Black Corvus made the Midnight Stone so that no feral line should ever die out, even if a feral had no children to inherit their powers.

"There are many shades of good and bad," said Quaker. "It rather depends on where you stand."

"Are you saying that the Spinning Man found a way to channel his spirit?" asked Caw. "To preserve himself, even after death?"

"I'm saying that if anyone can tell you how the spider feral endured, it would be Black Corvus himself," said Quaker.

Is this making sense to you? asked Shimmer.

Barely, said Glum.

I'm still waiting for cookies, said Screech. *He must have them somewhere—there are crumbs on the table.*

"But how can I talk to Black Corvus?" said Caw.

"You search for him," said Quaker. He nodded at the cloth-wrapped stone in Caw's hand.

Well, I'm glad he's cleared that up, said Shimmer.

Caw slipped the threaded pouch off his neck and tipped the Midnight Stone gently onto the footstool. Its polished black surface reflected the room and Caw's face leaning over it.

"Touch it," said Quaker.

"Won't it take my powers away?" said Caw nervously.

"I think not," said Quaker. "The stone belongs to the crow line."

He thinks *not,* said Shimmer.

Hardly reassuring, said Glum.

"If Black Corvus is in there, perhaps he will find you," said the cat feral.

Listen, Caw, said Shimmer. *I'm not sure about this.*

"I have to do it," said Caw. "There's no other way to help Selina."

He reached out his fingers, paused, and then let them rest on the Midnight Stone. There was no sudden jolt or flash, but its jet-black surface was colder than he expected, almost icy. He drew back his hand, and his fingertips clung to the stone a moment longer before peeling off.

You okay? asked Shimmer.

Caw nodded, then touched it again. The cold spread

immediately up his fingers in soft bursts, as if the Midnight Stone was an icy beating heart. Caw resisted the urge to pull away again and closed his eyes.

"Control the stone," urged Quaker. "*Use* it."

The deathly cold was inching up Caw's arm, and numbness crept along with it. Caw could feel his blood pumping, yet being pushed back away from his frozen arm.

Where are you, Corvus? he whispered.

The Midnight Stone continued to force its ice into Caw's body, but he fought back with his mind. He focused on where his blood met the freezing pulse of the stone and felt the tides of cold and heat colliding with each other.

Corvus, he said. *Corvus.*

Caw's thoughts became a black swirl, a self composed entirely of will. Slowly, he felt the cold recede. As it did so, Caw thrust his spirit in its wake, down his arm, through his wrist, and into his fingers. And with a final burst of strength, he left his body and entered the Midnight Stone.

Suddenly, with a prickle across the back of his neck, he realized he was not alone.

9

Caw opened his eyes. He was in a different room entirely. The walls were dark wood panels, and a huge hearth was piled high with logs. A leather-topped desk with a quill and inkwell sat below a lead-paned window. It was oddly familiar, but Caw couldn't say why. Silver tankards lined a shelf, and his feet sank into a thick rug.

"Welcome, Jack," said a deep voice.

He turned to see a man dressed in black from head to toe, except for the white cuffs of his shirt, which peeked out from beneath a black velvet jacket. He even wore black leather gloves. Above a neatly trimmed black beard, dark eyes surveyed Caw with a haughty glare. It was neither friendly nor hostile—but strangely curious. And Caw had seen that face before.

"Black Corvus," he said.

The man inclined his head a fraction. "We are family, Jack, so you must call me by my real name—Thomas."

Now Caw remembered where he recognized the room from—the vision he had seen in the worm feral's lair. He had been shown this place at the time when all the ferals had sworn to bestow a fraction of their powers on the Midnight Stone. This felt different—although he was now actually in it, the room was somehow more vague, less distinct. Caw sensed that each time he turned to face something new, whatever he had just been looking at was evaporating.

"I found you," he said.

"Or I found you," said Black Corvus. "You are not the first, Jack. Come, walk with me."

His voice was stern, and Caw obeyed without question.

They descended a narrow set of creaking wooden stairs. At the bottom, Black Corvus unbolted a door and swung it open onto the outside world. A wide muddy street with timber buildings opposite. The smell of wood smoke in the air. Caw followed Corvus, who'd already set off across the street, but had to jump back as a horse-drawn carriage careered toward him. It rattled past on huge wooden-spoked wheels, flicking up mud from the churned ruts in the road. In the back, a woman in a pink bonnet and a man in a tall hat sat beside each other. The woman was looking Caw's way, but she showed no sign of seeing him. As the carriage rolled onward, Corvus beckoned at Caw to follow with a jerk of his chin.

Caw crossed the street, stepping over a pile of horse dung, and saw this world ripple and blur in his peripheral vision. He was here, but he was not. It was an image—but one that he could feel with all his senses—and he knew it could vanish in a moment. He looked back at the house he'd come from and saw a tall, timber building with upper windows that stuck out from the front, supported by wooden struts below. It looked quite grand.

"What is this place?" he asked as his eyes swept over the street. They passed a wooden chapel set back from the thoroughfare, a cockerel spinning slightly on its spire. Beside the church, through an open set of doors, Caw saw a man with a leather apron hammering a piece of glowing metal. The man stopped and nodded to Black Corvus, who tipped his hat in response. Again, Caw sensed that he was invisible here.

"This is Blackstone," said Corvus, pausing as a flock of sheep crossed their path.

"*When* is it?" said Caw, hurrying after him.

"The year is not exact," said Corvus. "Sometime around 1680. The Midnight Stone holds my memories, and this place is made from them. I'm glad you came, Jack."

"I need your help," said Caw.

"Then let us go somewhere where we can talk," said Corvus.

They passed a tavern and a stable yard, and a group of women coming out of a shop with dresses in the window. A boy crossed the street carrying a stack of bread rolls on a tray. Blackstone was a small but bustling place. A couple of men playing cards on a veranda tipped their hats to Black Corvus, and he waved back.

At the end of the street, a wooden bridge crossed a small river, and they climbed a hill between pastureland, where golden wheat shivered in the cool breeze. Caw followed as his companion strode up the incline. Caw was panting a little as they reached the top, where a single tree stood, its branches sprawling over a small well.

"What is it you want from me?" said Corvus, sitting on the wall of the well.

"I need to help my friend," said Caw.

Corvus stared out over the town below them. It really was tiny—perhaps thirty buildings with fields beyond them as far as the eye could see. He sighed. "The White Widow."

"How do you know?" said Caw.

"I sense things—through the stone. It is a prism between this world and yours. Important things can penetrate." He paused. "Like evil."

"There must be a way I can free her," said Caw, shivering as the wind became colder still.

"There is not," said Black Corvus. He turned, his black eyes fixing on Caw. "Do not underestimate the tenacity of the spider line, Jack. They never stop weaving their vile webs. They hate us and always have. And the White Widow hates you too. She will not rest until you are dead."

"But it's the Spinning Man who hates me, not Selina," said Caw. "Somehow he's possessed her—*made* her into the White Widow."

"The name of your enemy is not important," said Black Corvus.

"All spider talkers are evil. That is what you need to know." He stood and took the wooden cover off the top of the well.

"But . . ."

"Come," said Corvus, pointing into the depths. "You will see."

Caw edged up and peered over the rim. Black water reflected his face for a moment, reminding him of the surface of the Midnight Stone. Then Corvus reached across, a pebble in hand, and dropped it. As the ripples spread, an image formed in the liquid, made of shadow and light but completely clear.

A child pressed into the corner of a room, spiders coming at him from every side as an old man stood over him, cackling. Another pebble splashed into the surface, and the vision changed to a woman lying pale and still in an ornate bed as spiders crept over her dresser and carried off a jeweled necklace on their backs. "What is this?" asked Caw.

"History," said Black Corvus. "The spider line is rotten to its core. It is our job to stamp it out for good."

Caw looked into Corvus's dark gaze. "But I can't kill my friend."

Corvus laid a hand on his shoulder and squeezed firmly. "You don't understand. She's already dead, Caw. She is like prey trapped in a silk cocoon, being slowly consumed. From the moment the Spinning Man took her, he has been sucking her life force away. Soon he will be powerful enough to exist without her."

"What do you mean?" asked Caw with a shudder.

"I mean she is only his temporary vessel," said Corvus. "He will drain her body, leaving an empty husk. And then he will rise again, in the flesh."

Caw shook his head fiercely. "That can't be true. The Spinning Man is dead."

"While his spirit lives, he will find a doorway back," said Corvus. "The girl is that doorway. You have my sympathy, Caw. I have lost enough friends to the spiders to know how you feel." He handed Caw a pebble.

Caw took it and dropped it over the well. As it sank beneath the water, he saw another image—spiders swarming across a woman and a man who writhed and then fell. *My parents.*

Caw looked away. "That was the Spinning Man, not the White Widow," he said.

"They are one and the same," said Corvus. "You have a duty, Jack. You must spare your friend more misery. *End the spider line forever.* For us, for your mother, and for every other feral who lives a life of goodness."

Caw felt sick. He steadied himself against the well and watched the water swirl below. His stomach churned and he closed his eyes, but water still seemed to fill his vision.

"Caw?" said a voice that didn't belong to Corvus. He peered down and saw another face in the water, blurred and indistinct.

The cold breeze was gone from the back of his neck; Caw realized the vision was releasing him. He felt a hard surface beneath his face, arms shaking him, then a hot sting across his cheek.

He blinked and a jowly face glared down at him. Felix Quaker's hand was raised for another slap. Caw was back in the attic flat, the room swaying nauseatingly around him. He drew his hand back from the Midnight Stone.

"About time!" said the cat feral.

The crows were squawking furiously.

"What's going on?" asked Caw.

At last! Glum said. *We thought you'd had your brain sucked out.*

Caw felt horribly disoriented. The Crow's Beak was lying on the table—*it wasn't there before, was it*? Then he remembered his earlier command back at the power plant. Krak and the others must have brought it here. "What time is it?" he mumbled.

"You've been out for nearly two hours," said Quaker.

Caw blinked hard. It felt like no more than ten minutes since he had laid his hand on the stone. "I spoke to Black Corvus," he said.

And? said Shimmer. *What did he say?*

Caw looked at each of his crows. "He said there was nothing we could do now that Selina is the White Widow."

Oh, said Shimmer.

"He said the Spinning Man was using her," said Caw. "That

there was a way for him to come back for real, as himself."

"There you are, then," said Quaker. The cat feral was frowning severely.

"Is everything okay?" asked Caw.

"You tell me," said Quaker. He pointed to the corner of the room, where a pigeon lay dead on the floor, missing several clumps of feathers. "My cats found it spying," Quaker spat. "Who else knows you're here?"

"No one," said Caw. "At least, I thought so."

Quaker paced angrily to the bed and pulled out a suitcase from underneath it. "I knew I shouldn't have gotten involved. All I wanted was somewhere I could live in peace. Why couldn't you leave me alone?" He began to stuff clothes into the open case.

"So that's it?" Caw said. "You're off?"

Quaker paused with his back to Caw as cats gathered around his feet. "I didn't want any of this," he said, then crossed to the door. "I'm settling up with the landlord." And then he was gone.

Screech landed on Caw's shoulder. *Hey, boss,* he said.

"If you're going to ask about cookies again, please don't," said Caw.

Listen, said Screech, sounding more serious than Caw had ever heard him. *You know I'd follow you anywhere. . . .*

"Screech, you're as loyal as they come," said Caw.

But this . . . it seems different. I mean—you killed *him, but now he's back. I just think it might be better—*

"What do you want me to do?" said Caw impatiently.

Screech raised one wing—a nervous twitch. *Maybe we should bury the hatchet with the other ferals,* he said. *We could handle it on our own, but strength in numbers, right? At least until we know what we're dealing with . . .*

Caw shrugged, and Screech tumbled off, landing on the floor.

"Not yet," said Caw. He wrapped up the Midnight Stone and sheathed the Crow's Beak. "I need to think."

You got it, Screech said. *You know I'm with you. Whatever happens.*

Morton and another crow dropped through the skylight and fluttered onto the table, looking agitated.

"What's going on?" said Caw.

The new crow hopped from side to side. *Spiders everywhere!* she cried. *Back at the power plant. We're under attack!*

The rubbish dump was no longer a lifeless landscape of trash. Spiders swarmed across it like a plague. They must have taken the crows by surprise, creeping up from beneath, because several birds were pinned, flapping on the ground, trying to break free.

Soaring above in the grip of his crows, Caw saw Krak rise on weak wings, then collapse again. Other crows swooped and dive-bombed, trying to pick the spiders off, only to rise covered in spiders themselves.

Glum, Screech, and Shimmer swooped down from the sky as Caw swept overhead. The spiders were everywhere. Caw told the crows who were carrying him to descend, and his feet crushed spiders as he hit the ground. He stamped through the melee, snatching up crows where he could, knocking the spiders from their wings, and tossing his birds up into the safety of the air. His hands were stinging with bites, and he could feel the spiders crawling under his clothes.

"Retreat!" he shouted.

Save yourselves! yelled Morton, but as one wave of crows lifted off, still more seemed trapped on the ground. Caw saw webbing across their backs, between their feathers—even over their eyes. This was no aimless attack. This was planned carnage.

And then he saw a movement high up on the wall of the old power plant.

Something pale darting through a window.

The White Widow.

Caw called crows to him and sprang off the ground in their grip, spiders tumbling from his body. He ignored the pricks of pain as the arachnids bit him, focusing on the power plant. But soon he couldn't see anything as spiders crawled over his face and he had to claw at his skin to scrape them off.

At last the crows carried him through the window of the derelict building—into a huge turbine hall. Huge metal bars crisscrossed the empty space, and the ground below was littered with rubble. Caw swept back and forth, eyes scanning the building's corners. There was no sign of the White Widow. He passed through another window and rose toward the roof.

They're retreating! Caw heard Shimmer cry.

As his crows carried him back to the scrapyard, he saw the last of the spiders vanishing through gaps in the rubbish, sinking out of sight like black water seeping into sand. They left countless injured crows in their wake flapping weakly or hobbling upright. Caw didn't know what to think. Why had the White Widow called off her forces?

Circling crows gradually came to land, to tend to the rest of the flock.

Only one bird was still in the air as Caw stood in the center of this nightmarish scene.

Where's Screech? said Glum, swooping back and forth. *Screech!*

Caw scanned the dump for his loyal lieutenant. He spotted a small gathering of crows beside a large pool of stagnant water. They stood facing the same way, completely motionless. And in the pool of dirty water there was something floating on its side. Something black, like a rag.

Caw started to run across the mounds of discarded rubbish. He tripped and fell, then scrambled up and ran again. A long keening call that he had never heard before echoed in his ears. The terrible cry of a crow that he knew came from Glum.

Shimmer swept past, crying out, *No . . . no . . .*

And the crows stood aside as Caw reached the pool. He waded straight in, his heart bursting in the hope that he was wrong but his head telling him that he wasn't.

Cupping his hands, he scooped Screech's lifeless body from the water.

10

A cruel wind whipped across the rubbish dump, tugging at Caw's freezing, sodden clothes and ruffling the feathers of his crows. He cradled Screech in his hands—a deadweight. The young crow's head hung limply, and his talons were curled. His eyes had already taken on a milky vagueness within their black depths, like a premonition of the Land of the Dead.

Glum had turned away, unable to look. Shimmer was talking to the older crow in a low voice that Caw couldn't hear. The other crows watched their master with unblinking eyes. He sat heavily, sitting cross-legged with the body laid in his lap, and he began to cry.

Screech had been with him since almost the start. He was the first crow Caw had really understood, the first who had brought him half a sandwich instead of a wriggling worm. They had grown up together, like brothers, and while Caw had gone from a five-year-old to an adolescent, Screech had stayed the same—funny, smart, reckless, and *loyal*. Caw had always known that Screech would have flown into fire for him. He would have given his life.

And now he had.

Screech had never once shied from danger. He had followed Caw everywhere, even when Caw had asked him not to. He was always at his master's side.

"He can't be gone. He just can't."

Oh, Caw, said Shimmer.

Caw hadn't realized he'd spoken aloud. Shimmer skipped onto his knee and lowered her head to press it against Screech's. They hadn't always seen eye to eye, but their rivalry was a fond one. Screech had liked to show off, and Shimmer enjoyed putting him in his place.

The crows are saying he rescued three others before the spiders overwhelmed him, she murmured.

Caw managed to suppress the sob that rose up at her words. He kept expecting Screech's wings to flutter, to hear his irrepressible voice—*Fooled you!*

But Screech didn't even look like himself anymore.

Caw wiped his eyes and looked over at Glum. The old crow was staring vacantly into the distance. "Glum?" he said.

Glum turned, his shoulders hunched. *I told you we couldn't do this alone!* he said. *Screech tried to tell you as well.*

Caw was taken aback. "I didn't know this would happen. I—I thought we were safe here."

Glum shook his beak angrily. *We'll never be safe from the*

spiders, he said. *You thought because you beat the Spinning Man once, you could beat him again. Alone.*

"No!" said Caw. "I just wanted to help Selina."

Glum made a disgusted sound. *Your arrogance killed Screech.*

Glum, that's not fair, said Shimmer. *Caw—*

But Glum was already hopping away across the rubbish.

"Glum, wait!" said Caw.

Let him go, said Shimmer. *Give him time.*

Caw sighed. If Screech had been like his brother, then the young crow had been like a son to Glum. Crows didn't have family like humans, but the deep love Glum had for Screech had been poorly disguised in his good-natured grumbling.

And he did have a point.

If Caw had done things differently, would Screech still be alive?

Don't listen to him, said Shimmer, as if reading Caw's thoughts. *He's just upset.*

Her words did nothing to soften the pain. Caw wondered if Shimmer really thought the same thing as Glum, deep down. And what about the other crows? For years he'd grown up with only three at his side and no idea he could command the whole flock. The changes had happened so fast that Caw realized he sometimes took them for granted. Would the crows always follow him blindly, or did their loyalty have limits?

He looked back to the window through which he'd chased the pale figure. "I think she was here—the White Widow," he said. "Watching."

Then why didn't she finish us off? said Shimmer.

Caw's sorrow hardened. "The Spinning Man is punishing me," he said. "He's not happy just to kill me. He wants to hurt me too. That's why the spiders went after Screech."

Shimmer was quiet for a moment. *You should let the crows look after him now,* she said. *They have a place they can take him.*

Caw nodded mutely.

It was one of the strange things about the crows that they never left their dead to the elements. It was practically unheard of to find a dead crow on the ground. Where they took them was a mystery, and one that Caw understood he was not supposed to question.

He laid Screech on the ground, and slowly a circle of crows gathered around.

Wait! said Shimmer. *What's that?*

The crows stepped back.

Caw peered in. "What?" he said. Despite everything, he dared to hope they'd made a mistake—that by some miracle Screech was still alive.

But the body was completely still.

In his talons, muttered Shimmer. *He's holding something.*

She nudged Screech's balled claws with her beak, and Caw saw something white wriggle inside. A spindly leg poked out.

"It's a spider!" he said.

The rest of the crows stalked menacingly.

Kill it! said one.

Let's rip it to pieces, added another. *One leg at a time.*

Caw put his hand over Screech's body. "No one touches it."

He gently pried Screech's talons apart, and the spider dropped onto the ground on its back. It was bone-white, and Caw's blood ran cold.

It rolled over and began to scramble away.

I want it! said a crow, and stabbed with its beak.

Caw brushed the crow aside. "I said leave it alone!"

The spider didn't seem sure which way to go, as each time it darted one way a crow blocked its path.

Why are you protecting it? said Shimmer.

It poisoned Screech! said Krak. *It's a killer.*

The spider lifted its front legs and spread its fangs defiantly. It was bigger than the last time Caw had seen it, several weeks before, but he somehow knew it was the same one. It was the bone-white spider he'd first spotted in the graveyard where his parents were buried, outside Blackstone, not long after his fight with the Spinning Man in the Land of the Dead.

The crows bustled, their eyes greedy and bright. Caw noticed an old plastic bottle lying on the rubbish heap nearby. He reached over, grabbed it, and unscrewed the lid. Holding the open neck beside the spider, he used the lid to coax it inside.

What are you doing? said Krak. *That's the enemy.*

Caw stood up, screwing on the lid and inspecting the spider now trapped in the bottle. It was Quaker who had first told him that unnaturally white creatures, like Caw's old crow Milky, were those that had somehow come back from the Land of the Dead. Could this spider be the same?

The crows were watching him, and for the first time he felt a twinge of dislike in their black stares. "Take care of Screech," he said, unable to keep an edge of anger from his voice.

The crows shuffled around the dead body, and some of them placed their talons carefully on Screech's wings, lifting him like coffin bearers. With a couple of flaps, the body was airborne, and the other crows followed in a tight formation. With Shimmer standing beside him, Caw watched them disappear into the clouds.

He pushed away his grief. The time to mourn his friend properly would have to come later.

"I need to speak to Quaker again," he said. "If we hurry, we might catch him."

Shimmer cocked her head. *You sure he'll be happy to see you?*

Caw could only shrug. What choice did he have?

Oh, great! said Shimmer. *Foxes.*

Caw saw them—a pair of russet shapes on the next roof over from Quaker's place. He sensed the weariness in the crows' wings as they banked, carrying him closer to the building. Whether it was because of the battle at the dump or the loss of so many, he couldn't tell. They had obeyed him—flocking as normal to lift him skyward—but he wondered what they were thinking now. How far he could count on them to follow.

They swooped over the skylight, and Caw caught the tiniest glimpse of a person in the room below. It was Johnny Fivetails, rifling through Quaker's meager possessions. So the good ferals had tracked Quaker down too. If they were here, it meant they were looking for Caw.

What do we do? asked Shimmer.

Was Lydia here too? Caw wondered. Pip?

His thoughts brought back the painful memory of the confrontation at the parking lot. Lydia's mother had sided with Johnny Fivetails, hadn't she? They were old friends. They had history. Caw spotted a dead cat lying against the side of the building, the white fur of its throat bloodied.

Oh no, muttered Shimmer. She must have seen it too. *You think a fox did that?*

"Or a coyote," said Caw.

Either way, Johnny and Velma Strickham clearly weren't just

paying Quaker a friendly visit.

"They'll try to take the Midnight Stone again," said Caw.

So where to? asked Shimmer.

Caw's head was spinning. He commanded his crows to take him to the only place he could think to go.

Blackstone Library was a shadow of its former self, its huge grand windows boarded up and the grass verges outside overgrown. Scraps of rubbish littered the steps, and graffiti scrawls covered the walls. A ribbon of yellow crime-scene tape was tangled in the branches of a young tree nearby. It was a reminder of the horror Caw had witnessed inside, only a few weeks ago.

They landed at the side of the building, beside the steps that led down to the bathroom window. It was covered with boards, but Caw managed to tug them free. He climbed through and Shimmer followed.

"No one will look for us here," he said.

It was cold inside the main hall, and the only light came from a couple of grubby windows high up in the dome that topped the building. The shelves were almost empty. Only a few books remained, scattered across the floor among discarded paperwork. The whole place smelled musty and decayed.

Caw hadn't visited the library since the day he and Lydia had found Miss Wallace, the librarian, murdered by the Spinning Man's thugs. She wasn't a feral, she had played no part in their war—she was just a kind woman who had taken pity on Caw, lending him books and giving him the occasional cup of hot chocolate.

Caw took off his jacket and emptied the pockets. He placed the spider bottle on a reading desk and then paused, staring around at the empty shelves. A pang of grief flooded his body. When Miss Wallace had been in charge, the library had been warm and cozy, hushed and peaceful, with everything in perfect order.

But now she was dead. Another innocent victim who had suffered because of Caw.

He had done this. Just like Screech. Just like Lydia's dog, Benjy, killed by one of Mamba's snakes. Everywhere Caw went, death followed, and he just kept running away. He was no better than Quaker. No—he was *worse*. Quaker had no choice, but Caw did. The solution was staring him in the face. Corvus had tried to tell him, but as usual Caw had tried to avoid the truth.

He looked at his hands, blue with cold and covered in throbbing spider bites. He flexed them, then let them curl into fists, squeezing so tight he felt the pulse of his blood right through to his fingertips. A throb of anger and hate.

Time to take control.

End this.

"Corvus was right," he said.

Shimmer cocked her head. *What do you mean?*

Caw took a deep breath. His chest felt warm, his skin on fire. "About the White Widow," he said. "Enough is enough. She's the spider feral now. That's all that matters."

From the bottle, the trapped spider watched him with its white stare. And a thought hit Caw like a truck.

Maybe it's been watching me all along.

He hesitated, frowning.

What's up? said Shimmer.

Caw's skin prickled as he began to piece it all together. Was that what the Spinning Man had meant in the psychiatric hospital? Caw had barely paid attention at the time, but it made sense.

And what about *when* he had first seen the spider: in the grave-yard, the day after he and Lydia had returned from the Land of the Dead. Caw had thought it was only the two of them who came back into the real world. But a small spider could easily have crept through as well.

He'd never have noticed.

That had to be it.

Following him. *All this time.*

At the Church of St. Francis, where Crumb had lived. *At my house.* On the roof of Cynthia Davenport's apartment . . .

The spider watched defiantly—its tiny body radiating malice that hit Caw in waves.

Earth to Caw! said Shimmer.

"Johnny Fivetails was right," Caw muttered. "The Midnight Stone made Selina the way she is. When she was on the apartment roof, she was holding the stone. But it wasn't just any spider that touched her." He pointed at the bottle. "It was that one. *He's* inside it. The spirit of the Spinning Man."

Caw grabbed the bottle, his heart racing.

Caw, wait! said Shimmer.

"I should have listened to the crows!" Caw shouted, unscrewing the lid. "I should have let them kill you!"

Caw tipped the bottle upside down and shook it hard. The spider dropped onto the floor. Caw lifted his boot and brought it down with a thud that echoed in the cavernous library.

Well, that's one way of dealing with it, said Shimmer.

Caw's rage began to subside, but he felt no satisfaction. He raised his foot to look at the broken body.

It wasn't there.

"Where's it—"

He felt a stab of pain on his ankle.

Where's the spider? said Shimmer.

Caw reeled as a wave of dizziness swept over him.

Caw, stay still! said Shimmer.

He saw a chair and stumbled toward it, but his feet seemed to belong to someone else, and he couldn't feel the floor beneath them anymore. His legs folded and he fell to one knee.

Caw? said Shimmer.

"Help me," mumbled Caw, and his fear spiked as he struggled to breathe. His throat was tight and burning. He clawed at his neck, feeling the pressure build in his chest.

Am I having a heart attack?

He fell flat on his face and saw Shimmer in front of him, flapping and squawking. "Help . . . ," he croaked again. His fingers slid into the pouch around his neck and closed over the Midnight Stone. Then his vision darkened and the world shrank.

Everything went black.

11

He floated over Blackstone, at the mercy of the air currents. He was neither boy nor crow, but something more ephemeral—a spirit, maybe. He felt weightless as the currents carried him over the sinuous coils of the Blackwater River, high above the twinkling yellow lights of the highways. Up ahead, the windows of the financial district towers sparkled silver and black. There was movement on the roof of one of them. A helicopter rose with spinning blades into the sky. Crows circled—thousands of them. And among them he saw a boy in ripped black clothing, holding the Crow's Beak and standing over the fallen Mother of Flies. A girl crouched beside her, shielding her mother's body.

The dream pulled him closer and he saw, as clear as a single star in the black tapestry of night, a small white spider on Selina's neck. It sank its fangs into her skin and she collapsed. The Midnight Stone rolled from her hand. He saw himself—the boy on the roof—rush to catch her, and then the crows swirled around, blocking the vision.

As they broke apart again, Caw's spirit was somewhere entirely different.

Above a wood that stretched for miles—though in the distance he saw a city sprawl. Blackstone? Perhaps. He dived into the woodland canopy, leaves whipping at his face. Branches shot past as he weaved between them at breakneck speed. He darted between trunks, and though he wanted to close his eyes, he couldn't. At any moment he expected to collide with unforgiving wood, but he did not. Then he burst into a clearing and slowed. A figure stood in the center, where moss had claimed the carcass of a falling tree, and moonlight cast everything in ghostly shadow.

It was a young woman. She wore a long, cream-colored coat, and her hair hung in a single dark lock that looped over her shoulder. She carried a handbag at her side. He saw delicate features and strong black brows—and his heart leaped. It was his mother, many, many years before. She looked so young she might not even have been twenty years old. Her head jerked up, but not toward him.

Someone else stepped into the clearing.

A young man, dressed in a black suit with a white shirt open at the chest, his black hair combed straight back, revealing a widow's peak. *The Spinning Man.* In addition to his youth, there was something ever so slightly odd about him that Caw couldn't place.

He looked to his mother again. Why wasn't she running? She didn't even look afraid.

As the Spinning Man strode toward her, she reached out her arms. Caw hung in the sky, shaking with disbelief.

The young man and woman linked hands for a moment and spoke a few words Caw couldn't hear. Then she opened the handbag and took out a box the size of an apple. Caw's mother unclipped its catch and opened it toward the spider feral. Caw saw the Midnight Stone gleaming inside. The moonlight caught its surface, and it reflected the glimmer of excitement in the Spinning Man's face. And now Caw understood why he looked so strange. It was the eyes. Caw had always seen them as black wells of hate, but the eyes of this young man were normal, brown irises set in white—kind, even. The Spinning Man reached out with his long, pale fingers, but Caw's mother closed the box again.

What was this? Why would his mother have shown her most treasured possession to their mortal enemy? She had broken the vow of the crow line. The vow to keep the Midnight Stone a secret . . .

The dark clouds above sped up momentarily as the trees rustled and a red sun broached the horizon, throwing spokes of purple and golden light across the forest. The burning orb rose quickly, fading from red to orange, then yellow, and the sky became pristine blue. Caw heard laughter and the tinky-tonk chimes of a fairground ride, and then the forest vanished.

He was sitting on a branch in a park. Flowers bloomed in pretty beds, and a fountain tossed sparkling columns of water into an ornamental pool. He jumped from the branch and swooped over neatly mown grass, past a set of open gates where wrought-iron letters spelled out *Blackstone Park*.

It was nothing like the park he knew—an abandoned, lonely place where no one ever ventured. In this vision, it was alive with families dressed in old-fashioned clothes, bonnets and breeches. Women carried brightly colored parasols, and some children were playing with a little dog that scampered back and forth.

Caw's flight took him to a bench where an old man sat. In front of him, three children watched openmouthed as he held his hands in front of them. Caw saw cotton threads suspended between his fingers. No—they were too thin for that, too delicate. And there were insects scurrying along them.

Silk webs.

A spider feral . . .

One of the children came closer and dropped a coin into the old man's hat, which lay before him on the ground. He nodded kindly and the children ran away giggling. The man flicked a glance at Caw and smiled. Then a gust of air snatched Caw upward and carried him away.

As he rose above the park, he saw the city once more, but a shrunken version. Gone were the prison and the skyscrapers, gone the industrial sprawl south of the river. Wide avenues with grand houses rattled with horses and carts. Caw flew into the garden of one of them, landing on a low wall overgrown with weeds, where two identical young girls were holding hands and spinning around. Faster and faster they went until momentum broke them apart and they toppled into the grass. One rushed to the other, holding out a hand. As they touched, a column of spiders crisscrossed their fingers and they both giggled. They waved at Caw, showing gap-toothed grins.

The girls and the house vanished and Caw found himself standing on the stone wall of a well, under a tree. Once more he was looking down at the old Blackstone that Corvus had brought him to. It was nighttime. Caw was alone.

He heard a noise—a scream—and turned away from Blackstone, gazing across the fields. Gray corn swayed. Beyond the expanse of crops, Caw glimpsed a flicker of fire. He took off from the well and glided across the fields. He made out an isolated barn squatting in the corner of a far-off field, and flaming torches. They were moving in a procession toward the building, and Caw saw them slip inside. Circling the barn once, he saw a small half-open hatch on the upper floor, under the eaves. He flew inside, landing on one of the rough-hewn beams that supported the roof.

Below him, the people carrying the torches had formed a circle around a woman. Her face was bruised and swollen and she was limping. One of the group stepped forward and backhanded her across the cheek. Caw gasped. It was Black Corvus.

"If you see any of her spiders, burn them," said Corvus to his companions.

"Please . . . ," said the woman. "I've done nothing wrong, Thomas."

Corvus's lip curled in a sneer. "Don't lie to us," he said.

"Who made you our leader anyway?" said the woman.

Corvus raised his hand again and she cowered back. Then he turned to a man with a torch and nodded. The man leaned his head back and howled.

The door to the barn swung open and another man staggered through, two wolves snapping at his heels. The woman shrieked.

"Mary!" cried the man. He tried to run toward her, but one of the wolves grabbed at his trousers and he fell headlong to the floor. The bruised woman took a step toward him, but Black Corvus thrust her back and two others from the circle seized her arms. She struggled but couldn't break free.

Corvus stood in front of her. "You stand accused, spider talker, of sharing the secrets of the ferals. How do you plead?"

"He's my husband!" she shrieked. "Please, he won't tell anyone else."

"Then I find you guilty," said the crow feral. "Our secrets must be guarded. Under pain of death."

"What have you become, Thomas?" said the woman. "All

because I chose someone else—is that why you punish us?"

"Not another word!" said Corvus. "You are not worthy of my protection."

The woman turned to the others in the group. "We are supposed to be allies. Friends! Matthew? Mr. Cooper? Rebecca? I beg you—stop this madness!"

But each of them looked away.

Corvus turned from her and strode toward the man being guarded by wolves. He lifted both hands to the ceiling, as if reaching to grasp the sky. The two wolves padded away to join a bearded man in the circle. Caw felt the presence of many crows above, gathering over the rafters. He sensed the weight of their anger, and a terror filled him.

Black Corvus clenched his fists and pulled them toward his chest. Crows flooded through the open hatch into the barn, a shrieking stream of flapping feathers and snapping beaks. They descended on the man below. Mary's screams mixed with those of her husband as he writhed on the ground, blood streaking down his hands as he tried to bat the birds away. The rest of the gathering looked on, flinching, or turned away. Only Black Corvus stood still, unblinking eyes fixed on the horrifying spectacle.

To his relief Caw felt himself rising out of the barn, haunted by the ever-weaker sounds of the assaulted man. At last there was a silence, broken only by the woman's sobs.

Black Corvus came out of the barn and his crows ascended to the sky, their terrible duty done. The rest of the ferals followed, the last two dragging the shuddering, semiconscious spider feral from the scene.

"Take her to the asylum," said Corvus. "No one will believe her crazed stories there."

Caw watched the ferals set off along the track, back toward the town. Only Black Corvus stayed behind, holding a torch, half his face bathed in red light.

Was this miscarriage of justice what the Spinning Man had referred to, back at the psychiatric hospital, when he spoke to Caw and Lydia? He'd told them that a spider feral had died in that ancient brick-walled cell—a spider feral who wasn't mad.

Black Corvus tossed his flaming torch into the barn. Caw saw orange flicker as the fire caught hold, and smoke began to billow out of the door. It wasn't long before flames licked up the timber walls.

There are many shades of good and bad, Quaker had said.

Caw rose again, but a crow blocked his path. Suddenly there were hundreds of them, coming at him from every side. Each way Caw turned, he was buffeted by wings, knocked this way and that. He tried to climb, but the murder of crows forced him lower. The ground rushed toward him and he struck it hard, tumbling several times, then coming to rest on the dusty earth.

As he turned over, he saw Black Corvus standing above him. Caw tried to scramble away, but Corvus seized him around the throat and hauled him upright. Caw's spirit had taken human form at the worst possible moment. Strong fingers cut off his airway and he couldn't breathe. Black Corvus lifted Caw off the ground, his face full of hate.

"What are you doing here, Jack?" he snarled.

12

The burning barn vanished, and in its place Caw saw a fire blazing in a hearth. Black Corvus released him, and he dropped to timber floorboards in a heap. They were back in Corvus's study. Every sense told Caw he was in danger—the very air seemed laced with threat.

"You killed that man," said Caw, massaging his throat. "Why?"

Corvus picked up a thick glass decanter from his desk and poured amber liquid into a glass. "You are in no position to question me," he said. "You have been communing with the spider line. *They* brought you here."

"I wasn't *communing* with anyone," said Caw. "A spider bit me."

Corvus swigged his drink and stabbed a gloved hand at Caw. "I told you, Jack. They're evil." He shook his head. "If only I could have found her child, we would have stopped the spider line forever that night."

"Mary—that woman—she didn't look evil," said Caw. "It looked like—like you were just jealous."

Black Corvus's eyes flashed darkly. "Careful what you say, Jack," he snapped. He took another sip and blinked slowly. "You are young and naive. She revealed our secret. She endangered all of us."

"She only told her husband. Why shouldn't she?"

"Because he was one of *them*!" spat Corvus. "How can you not understand? They despise us. They always have. Do you know how many ferals have been lynched or beaten or burned alive?"

"But what you did—that's just as bad," said Caw. "Your crows . . . they—they tore him to pieces."

"I don't have to explain myself," said Corvus. "Humans are weak creatures. We need them to continue our lines, but those who learn the truth always come to fear us, or to envy our powers. If all of humanity knew we existed, we ferals would soon be slaughtered. They are our enemies."

Caw stared at Corvus. "You sound like the Spinning Man," he said.

Black Corvus threw his glass at the hearth and it exploded into fragments. He advanced on Caw, who backed away, raising his arms to defend himself. But Corvus stopped short, face red and sweating. "I will forgive you that, Jack, because of the blood we share, but *do not* push me."

Corvus spun on his heel and strode to the window, surveying the town outside. "I have lived with this reality, this persecution,

163

my whole life, Jack," he said. "I have seen what humans are capable of. Our enemies must be dealt with . . . firmly. Now, have you killed the White Widow yet?"

Caw thought about the horror in the barn. If that was what Corvus meant by dealing with his enemies *firmly*, he wanted no part of it. Mary and her husband had done nothing wrong. And the other ferals had simply stood by, obeying Corvus without even a whimper of defiance, swallowing his twisted logic. But Caw saw through it. For all Black Corvus's talk of evil and justice and noble struggle, Caw now knew it was hatred that had driven him. *Petty, jealous hatred.*

Caw had almost fallen for his ancestor's act himself. He had almost given up on Selina. He had almost followed Black Corvus's command without questioning it.

"Well, boy?" snapped Corvus.

"No," said Caw. "And I never will."

Black Corvus turned around slowly, his eyes flashing with fury. "If you cannot kill her, you are not worthy to call yourself my heir. You are like your mother—a pitiable weakling and an embarrassment to our blood."

Caw felt his cheeks heating with anger. "You're the embarrassment," he said. "I'm ashamed to be descended from you."

"Get out!" growled Corvus, his voice dead and cold.

Caw frowned.

Corvus smashed a fist down on the table and roared so loud Caw felt the floorboards tremble. "Get out of my sight!"

Caw descended the steps, opening the door onto the street. The cold twilight air received him. Blackstone was dark—not a single candle glowed in any of the windows. The only illumination came from the moon, and even that was shrouded by cloud like a face hidden behind a veil.

Caw began to walk along the center of the street with no idea where he was headed. The ground squelched under his feet as he slipped in the mud. He knew he had done the right thing. Corvus was not the man he'd believed him to be. He was no hero at all. Caw looked left and right. The street seemed narrower than earlier.

"I've got to get home," he said aloud.

Silence.

The last time he'd been here, it was Quaker who'd brought him back to reality with a slap to the cheek. Caw closed his eyes and pinched himself on the arm, hard. But when he opened them again, he was in exactly the same spot.

The sign over the haberdashery creaked on its hanging chain. Caw sensed a shadow pass overhead and glanced up. It was Black Corvus, gliding smoothly across the sky, supported by crows. He landed in the middle of the road ahead.

"I've made up my mind, Jack," he said. "This ends now."

The sky blackened over the town as thousands of birds swept in from all directions. Caw watched them alight across the buildings on either side of the street. He hadn't summoned them himself, which could only mean one thing. Caw reached out with his mind, searching for any birds that might heed him.

"Let's see what you're capable of," said Black Corvus. He reached toward the general store and beckoned with one hand. The crows on its roof rose in the air. He pointed to the other side of the street and the birds there did the same. Then Black Corvus thrust both hands toward Caw, and the crows flew straight at him.

Caw called out to more of the crows and was relieved as a flock shot past him to meet the attack. The two murders were headed straight for each other, neither backing down. Caw held his birds steady.

But at the last moment his crows scattered and Corvus's birds shot through the gap. Caw tried to stop them with his mind, to slow them down, but he sensed the immense power of his ancestor behind their headlong rush. He threw up his arms and turned as crows crashed into him in an unstoppable wave. Talons and beaks ripped at his clothes, and Caw fell to the ground. The birds flew away, and he peered out to see them ascending into the skies again.

Corvus laughed. "Pathetic," he said.

Caw gritted his teeth and sent out a summons once more. He felt his scattered crows coalesce behind the town's bank and swing around as Corvus strode toward him.

"To think how my mighty line has fallen," said Black Corvus, shaking his head.

Caw pretended he couldn't stand, struggling on his knees as his crows leveled off in a low flight behind Corvus.

"What you don't understand," said Corvus, "is that feral power is easily gained but hard to keep." The crows were almost on him. Caw willed them to fly faster, to close the gap. . . .

"It must be earned, through trust," said Corvus. And with a wave of his hand, the crows at his back banked sharply to either side of him, two streams flitting harmlessly past. They fell across Caw's body instead and he was hoisted into the sky. The crows bore him higher, until he was at least twenty feet up in the air.

Black Corvus, alone in the middle of the street, stared up.

"This is the boy who let so many of you die at the hands of the spider feral!" he called. "He is a traitor to our line—a shameful stain on the honor of all crows. Show him how we treat traitors!"

Caw tried to reach into the crows' minds, but he sensed only a black and impenetrable wall. They carried him high above the buildings, until he could no longer see Black Corvus's face clearly. He could feel his ancestor's spirit—the crows throbbed with his malevolence.

Then the crows holding Caw's left arm unhooked their talons, and he lurched downward.

"No!" Caw cried. "Please!"

"I'll show you the true power of the crow talker!" roared Black Corvus.

And as one, the remaining crows holding Caw aloft let go and he plummeted through the air. He twisted as he fell, trying to find his crow form, but it simply *wasn't there*. The roof of a building rushed toward him, and Caw closed his eyes, bracing himself for the impact. . . .

Caw jerked upright into a sitting position. The library shelves loomed all around him. Shimmer flapped and squawked. A wave of nausea made his head spin and he tried to stand, but his legs buckled. As he fell to his knees, pain gripped his insides and twisted. He retched.

It's poison, he remembered. *The spider's venom.*

He saw the white spider hanging from a bookshelf on a thread of silk, spinning slowly. He snatched for it, then fell flat on his face. More pain racked his shaking body as the spider scrabbled against his palm.

With his face pressed against the filthy carpet, he watched the spines of the books begin to swirl. He saw a white-haired figure flitting between the shelves. The White Widow. She paused and stared at him, smiling. Then her edges seemed to blur and she vanished.

Feet appeared at eye level and faces leered down.

Mrs. Strickham.

Crumb.

Johnny Fivetails.

"He's lost," said Crumb.

"No hope for him now," added Lydia's mother.

"Last of the crow line," said Johnny. "And to think, we all believed in him."

Caw tried to speak but couldn't form any words.

The heads of the ferals began to distort, then vanished.

Caw rolled onto his back, and the room blurred horribly out of focus. Shimmer hopped onto his chest, looking down. "Help me . . . ," Caw managed.

Shimmer cocked her head and looked at him strangely. Sounds were coming from her beak but no words. A bolt of despair struck Caw in the heart.

"Shimmer?" he said. "I can't understand you."

She squawked again and flew off.

"It's over, boy," intoned Black Corvus's voice, from somewhere in the distance. "I've taken them from you. You are the crow talker no more."

Jack Carmichael felt his mind untether, and he drifted into nothingness.

13

"Caw?"

His mouth tasted stale, and his eyelids were heavy, but he felt a coolness across his forehead.

"Caw, wake up."

It took a few seconds to place the voice.

He opened his eyes and saw Lydia leaning over him. In her hand was a damp cloth. He wondered if it was another vision. The room swam in and out of focus.

"Where am I?" he said.

"In the library. Glum led me here. Everyone's been looking for you, Caw."

Caw sat up, his head throbbing. Lydia placed a hand behind his back to support him.

"Glum?" he said. "Shimmer?"

"They're right here," said Lydia. "Where's Screech?"

It all came back in a rush that made Caw draw a shuddering breath.

"Caw, are you okay?"

Moisture sprang up in Caw's eyes. "Screech is dead," he said.

Lydia's hand shot to her mouth. Caw blinked away the tears. "Spiders got him."

Lydia lowered her hand, and he saw that her lip was trembling. "I'm so sorry," she said. "I . . . I don't know what to say."

Caw heard a crow call and saw Shimmer and Glum sitting on the desktop. The old crow opened his beak and warbled.

Caw shook his head. "No . . ."

"What is it?" asked Lydia.

Glum warbled again. Caw's heart pounded with a fear and sadness more profound than anything he'd felt before. *It can't be true. I can't have lost them.* But even Glum's eyes seemed different. Emotionless. Distant. Empty.

"Please, no . . . ," said Caw.

"You're frightening me," said Lydia. "Tell me what's wrong."

Caw looked into her face. How *could* he tell her? Even the words on the tip of his tongue were enough to make his heart shudder. He tried to speak, but all that came out was a wail. He buried his face in his hands.

"What's the matter?" demanded Lydia, her voice severe and afraid at the same time.

Caw looked through his fingers. Things would never be like

they were before. "I . . . I can't understand them," he said.

"Who?" said Lydia, but she must have known, because she glanced at Shimmer. The crow chirped softly, and the sound was like a kick to Caw's gut. *I've lost her. Lost them all.*

"Caw," said Lydia, gripping his arm. "Tell me what's happening so I can help."

"Black Corvus," said Caw quietly. "He took away my feral powers."

"How?" said Lydia, eyes wide.

"I don't know," Caw said. He could hardly look at her. Shame forced his gaze down.

"That doesn't make sense," said Lydia. "Black Corvus is your ancestor: your friend."

Caw shook his head. "He's not like we thought at all."

In faltering sentences, he tried to explain about the visions he'd seen at Quaker's, about entering the Midnight Stone. Lydia listened patiently and when he finished, Caw was close to crying.

Lydia put her arm around him. "It'll be all right," she said. "We'll get them back."

But Caw knew they couldn't. It wasn't supposed to happen like this—ferals only lost their powers when they died. He felt like a blind man who'd found his sight only to have it snatched away again. He couldn't bear it. What was he without the crows? *Nothing.* He'd lost *himself.*

"What's wrong with your hand?" asked Lydia.

Caw looked down and saw that his right hand was still balled in a fist. He flexed his fingers painfully, and something fell out to the floor.

"Urgh!" said Lydia.

It was the white spider, its legs tucked up. Caw must have crushed it to death.

"Where did you find that?" Lydia asked.

Caw shook his head. "Screech caught it, before . . ." He took a deep breath. Lydia put a hand on his shoulder. "Actually, I think it might have found me. It's from the Land of the Dead."

"Are you serious?" said Lydia.

Caw explained about the Spinning Man's spirit, and how it had found its way into Selina on the rooftop.

"And you saw all this . . . in a vision?" said Lydia.

Caw suddenly felt very tired. He realized that he hadn't slept since the night before last, when Pip's mice had brought them the information about the upcoming bank raid. Since then his world had turned upside down. The good ferals had pushed him out and he was fighting an enemy he'd thought was long dead. He glanced at Shimmer and Glum and felt a wave of despair. Even the crows— his oldest friends—were abandoning him. It was all happening just as the Spinning Man had promised.

Caw stood up and felt the Midnight Stone shifting against his chest. It gave him an idea. A shred of hope. He took a step toward the desk and Glum, holding out his hand.

Glum flapped in alarm and his wing beats stirred dust on the table. The crow took off.

"Come back," Caw pleaded.

Glum alighted on a high shelf out of reach. A moment later, Shimmer joined him. She watched Caw quizzically.

"Please," Caw said. He looked around and saw a stepladder. If he could just touch one of them and the Midnight Stone at the same time, maybe he could . . .

Both crows flew toward an upper window that was slightly ajar. They squeezed through the gap and vanished without a backward glance.

Caw sagged against the edge of the desk. "It's all fallen to pieces," he said.

For a time, there was silence. Every so often Caw looked at the window, praying his companions might reappear but knowing they would not.

Then Lydia cleared her throat. "Listen, Caw—the White Widow is still out there. I heard Mom and the others talking—they've got their animals scouring the city. We'll find her. If we all stick together, we can defeat her. I know we can."

"I can't," said Caw. "Don't you see? I'm nothing now. The crows—"

"Don't say that," said Lydia fiercely. "I can't control any animals, but I'm not nothing, am I?"

The anger in her face took Caw by surprise. "That isn't what I meant."

"Isn't it?" she said. "Caw, when I met you the first time, you were just a boy living in a tree with three birds. You didn't know you had any powers. You dressed in rags, you barely spoke, and frankly, you didn't smell very good either."

"So?" said Caw.

"*So*, I liked you just as much then as I do now," said Lydia. "The crows don't make you who you are, got it? You aren't nothing. You're my friend. And you always will be."

Caw swallowed. "Tell me what to do," he said.

Lydia pursed her lips and looked him in the eye. "Go back to the others," she said. "They want the same thing you do."

And Caw knew she was right. He gripped the cord hanging around his neck and tugged the pouch angrily into the open.

"What are you doing? What's that?" said Lydia.

"All along I've been protecting this because I thought that's what the crow ferals were supposed to do," said Caw. "I thought I was honoring a promise Black Corvus made. But we're the *last* people who should be trusted with it."

"I don't understand," said Lydia.

Caw snorted. "Black Corvus was cruel and he was jealous. He

hated people who weren't ferals. He was a bad person to the core."

"But you're not like that," said Lydia. "You're good, Caw. Anyone can see it."

"What about Johnny Fivetails?" asked Caw. "He couldn't see it. And neither could the others in that parking lot."

Every moment Caw felt more and more ashamed of how he'd acted. Keeping the Midnight Stone for himself was exactly the sort of thing Black Corvus would have done. To think that the coyote feral had returned to Blackstone expecting to meet a brave hero, and all he got was a boy who just ran away as soon as things got tough.

"Johnny's not perfect," said Lydia. "But he's on our side. They all are. Come on, let's go and find them." She offered Caw a hand.

Caw's heart was heavy. He felt childish. Lydia was right. Her mother, Crumb, the others—they were his friends. He had to stick to his own kind—

Only they weren't his kind now, were they? He wasn't a feral any longer.

Suddenly Lydia jumped back with a gasp. Caw followed her gaze and saw that the crushed white spider had begun to move. It clambered to its feet, then scurried toward a bookshelf.

"I thought I killed it," he said.

"Well, let's follow it!" said Lydia. She dropped to her knees and peered under the shelf.

"Why?" said Caw.

"Because," said Lydia. "Doesn't a spider always head back to its web? It might lead us to the White Widow."

"But Lydia, you have to understand. Killing her is exactly what Black Corvus wants," said Caw. "And I'm not going to do it. That's why he took away my powers."

Lydia looked at him, and he saw doubt flicker in her eyes. "What if we can't save her?" she asked.

"I have no idea," said Caw. "But if there's a way for the Spinning Man to infect her, there must be a way to cure her too." He said it with confidence, but he wasn't sure he believed it.

"It's on the move!" said Lydia, springing up. The spider scurried out from beneath the shelf, heading toward a barred door with heavy bolts. Somehow it squeezed underneath it, through an impossibly small gap.

"Don't lose it!" said Lydia, unfastening the bottom bolt. Caw took the one at the top and they shouldered through into the library parking lot. Caw saw the white spider scuttling past a bench.

It was moving quickly, but he and Lydia kept pace. Beyond the library, Blackstone became a warren of small streets that were increasingly busy. Caw looked up into the dimming sky. Half by instinct, he closed his eyes and desperately tried to find any crows. But his world felt empty.

The spider hesitated, tucked up against a wall, then set off down a street packed with pedestrians. No one seemed to notice the curious creature scuttling along—and several times their feet came dangerously close to crushing it. Caw and Lydia ran behind it, occasionally bashing into people and muttering apologies.

The spider leaped off the curb and headed across the road as cars swished past. Miraculously, the spider made it to the other side. A driver shouted angrily and another beeped his horn as Caw and Lydia wove in between the traffic.

Caw lost sight of the spider and started to panic, until Lydia grabbed his arm and tugged him toward a narrow passage between two shops. At the end of it they emerged into a quiet garden square with tall old buildings on each side. The spider scurried along the pavement, then headed up a set of white marble steps between two stone lions.

Caw slowed his pace.

"It's the Leo Hotel," said Lydia. "That's one of the most expensive places to stay in Blackstone." She looked at Caw. He knew what she was thinking. It didn't seem like the sort of place the White Widow would be staying. "Let's check it out," she said finally.

"Wait!" said Caw. "Are you sure?" He gestured to his clothes.

"We might not get another chance," said Lydia. "Come on!"

Caw followed her up the steps and into the hotel.

Quiet piano music tinkled across the spotless foyer. A chandelier dangled from the ceiling, throwing out shards of sparkling light. Beyond a few huge velvet sofas was the glass reception desk. A woman in a dark suit stood behind it, watching them as they entered. The white spider was nowhere to be seen.

"Hello. Can I help you?"

Caw felt painfully underdressed. If he said the wrong thing, they'd be thrown out very quickly indeed. "We're looking for someone," he said.

The receptionist's fixed smile remained, but it was getting less authentic by the second. She looked Caw up and down. "A guest, sir?"

"Of course," said Lydia bossily. "We're meeting someone. At five o'clock."

The clock behind the counter read 4:52. The receptionist stiffened and tapped the thin screen in front of her.

"What's the guest's name, please?" she said. "I can make a call to the room, unless the guest has requested not to be disturbed."

Caw glanced at Lydia, then spoke quickly. "Davenport," he said.

The receptionist didn't even look at the screen. "We have no one under that name staying at the hotel," she said.

"Really?" said Lydia. "Don't you need to check?"

"I do not," said the woman behind the desk. "Are you sure this is the correct hotel? There are some"—her lips curled—"other establishments nearby."

Lydia leaned on the counter. "Our friend is definitely staying at the Leo," she said. "She's quite private, though, so she might have booked under a different name." She pointed to the screen, which was half facing them. "If we could see a list of rooms—"

The receptionist turned the screen so they couldn't see it at all. "Quite impossible, I'm afraid. We have a strict privacy protocol at the hotel."

"Fine," said Lydia. "We'll just wait over there, then."

The receptionist looked far from happy. She glanced over her shoulder at the clock. "Five o'clock, you say?"

Lydia nodded and spun on her heel. Caw followed his friend across the foyer to the high-backed sofas, where they sank into soft velvet cushions.

"What now?" he whispered.

Lydia shrugged. "I've done my part. I've bought us eight whole minutes. Any ideas?"

Caw glanced in a mirror opposite them and looked at the stairs. The white spider could have gone anywhere. There was an elevator, but no way to get to it without being seen. He wondered how long they could wait before the receptionist asked them to leave.

"You think the White Widow is really staying here?" said Lydia.

Caw had to admit it seemed unlikely. But why else would the white spider have come to this place?

Unless it was deliberately leading us to a dead end.

He was about to say as much to Lydia when he heard a soft

chime, and the illuminated numbers above the elevator ticked down.

4...3...2...

L.

The elevator dinged and the doors slid open. Caw heard someone whistling a merry tune; then a man stepped out.

Caw caught his breath as Lydia drew in a soft gasp.

The man had sleek blond hair and was dressed in a white T-shirt, jacket, and jeans. He was wheeling a suitcase.

Johnny Fivetails.

Caw pressed himself back into the sofa. He could see the coyote feral in the mirror opposite, which meant that if Johnny looked that way, he could see Caw and Lydia too. But instead the coyote feral walked straight to the reception desk, with his back to them. "I'd like to check out, please," he said.

"Certainly, sir," said the receptionist. As she tapped on her screen, she glanced over toward the sofas. "You're not meeting anyone today?" she said.

Caw would have sworn his heart was beating loud enough to be heard. He met Lydia's eyes, open wide with fright, and saw she was gripping the armrest tightly.

Johnny looked up. "No. Why?"

The receptionist shook her head. "Apologies, sir, my mistake," she said, laying a piece of paper in front of him. "If you could sign at the bottom, please. How was your stay with us?"

"Very pleasurable," said Johnny, scribbling with a pen.

"You must accept our apologies for the state of your room," said the receptionist. "You'll see we've taken one night off the bill."

Johnny waved a hand. "Really, it's not a problem."

The receptionist shuddered. "I can tell you, sir—it's a long way below the standards we strive for. When our poor housekeeper saw those webs on the furniture, she was deeply disturbed."

"Not your fault," said Johnny. "Besides, I happen to rather like spiders."

He smiled as he held out his other hand, and Caw squinted to see what he was doing. Suddenly the receptionist jumped back with a shriek.

"It's quite all right," said Johnny. Caw's breath caught in his throat as he saw a small white creature scurrying across the coyote feral's knuckles. "This one's *very* friendly."

The receptionist had turned pale. "Have a good day, sir," she mumbled.

Caw's body felt as though it was welded to the seat. Lydia's face had drained of blood.

Johnny Fivetails had their white spider.

And that could only mean one thing.

14

Still smiling, the coyote feral picked up his case and strode out of the foyer. As soon as he'd gone, Caw leaped to his feet. "You're leaving?" called the receptionist.

Lydia nodded as she ran for the door. "You were right—wrong hotel!"

Without waiting for a response, they dashed down the steps, just in time to see Johnny Fivetails climbing into a taxi across the street. It pulled away at once and turned a corner.

"After him!" said Caw.

He ran to the public gardens and vaulted over the railings, trailed closely by Lydia. They sprinted across the grass—the taxi was almost at the far side of the square already.

"We'll lose it," puffed Lydia. As they jumped over the railings on the other side, she raised her hand. Another taxi swerved across the road and the driver wound down his window. "Yes, miss?"

Lydia pointed to Johnny's cab, edging around the corner. "Can you follow that taxi?"

"Are you serious?" said the driver.

Lydia fished in her pocket and pulled out several notes.

The driver nodded. "Hop in, then."

Caw and Lydia jumped into the back, and the driver set off after Fivetails's car.

"I don't get it," said Lydia, fastening her seat belt. "Why did he have the spider, unless he's . . ."

"Working with the Spinning Man," said Caw quietly. Out loud, it sounded even worse than it had in his head.

"But why?" asked Lydia.

"I have no idea," Caw replied.

A sick feeling swirled in Caw's belly as he remembered when he'd first met the coyote feral. Hadn't Johnny said he was staying in *some dump by the river*? So he'd been lying from the very start.

Caw's nausea swelled as he thought of Johnny charming all the other ferals at his house. All the smiles and the pats on the back—had they been fake? The way he'd shown up at the bank raid, just in the nick of time . . .

Caw flushed to think how he'd been taken in.

Just like with Black Corvus.

Caw had been so eager to please, to be liked, that he'd missed the truth about them both.

"We're near my house!" said Lydia, nudging Caw from his thoughts. He looked out of the window and saw they were approaching the road that looped around Blackstone Park. The street lamps had come on, and in their soft glow Caw spotted Johnny's taxi pulling over up ahead.

"Turn right here," said Lydia, and their cab steered into a side road. She paid the driver, and they climbed out and rushed to peer around the corner. The other cab had pulled away too, and Johnny Fivetails was striding along the sidewalk. When he reached the park, the coyote feral looked left and right, then took a run up and leaped, hooking his hands over the top of the park wall. He swung himself over and vanished inside.

Caw ran along the sidewalk to the park wall and scrambled up. Lying across the top, he reached down for Lydia and pulled her up too. The park was wreathed in shadow, with no one in sight. It was such a familiar place, yet somehow right now it seemed full of silent menace, the dark trees looming overhead. Caw sensed a flicker of movement and spotted a black cat prowling along the wall.

"What are you doing here?" muttered Caw as the cat approached and nuzzled his hand.

"Is it one of Quaker's?" asked Lydia.

Caw shrugged. It had no collar, but if it was a stray, it was well fed. The cat hopped off into the road and scampered away through the evening light.

Caw lowered himself from the wall into the shadows. Dried leaves crunched under his feet. Lydia slipped down beside him. The moon was already shining, silvering the leaves.

Caw scanned the park—if there were coyotes here, he and Lydia would be sniffed out quickly. With cautious steps, they crept from tree to tree.

It was strange being back here again. Though it had only been a month or so since this had been his home, it felt like something from another life. Screech, Glum, and Milky had been there with him always, as constant and reliable as the changing of the seasons. For a moment, a shock of grief made it hard to breathe.

Stay focused, he told himself. *For Screech. For the past.*

Lydia picked up a fallen branch and gripped it in both hands like a baseball bat. Caw drew out the Crow's Beak. He couldn't imagine what the coyote feral was doing here, but he doubted that Johnny would be pleased to see him.

They passed the rusted swings and deserted playground, then skirted the old pavilion and bandstand. Caw remembered the bright colors of the Blackstone Park he had seen in his vision, and the kindly spider feral entertaining children. He didn't want to believe it, but he knew in his heart that what he had seen was real. Spider ferals, young and old, leading good lives.

Lydia stopped and grabbed Caw's shoulder, pushing him down. She pointed through the trees. Caw saw Johnny Fivetails sitting on the edge of the old fountain—it had been dry as long as Caw had known, the statue of nymphs at its center flaking and forgotten.

Johnny had a cigarette between his lips, and its smoke looped up into the branches above.

Caw's eyes searched the darkness on either side of the fountain. He saw no sign of any coyotes, but that didn't mean they weren't there.

"What now?" whispered Lydia. Johnny seemed in no hurry to move. "I think he's waiting for—"

The coyote feral stood up suddenly, tossing down the cigarette and crushing it beneath his boot. He was looking upward, and for a mad moment Caw dared to hope that his crows had returned, circling overhead. But only a moth fluttered down, swirling around Johnny's head.

Then another.

And another.

The coyote feral shook his head irritably and the moths landed on his shoulders.

"Enough games," said Johnny. "Come out where I can see you."

"Beautiful, aren't they?" said a well-known voice.

The stone nymphs of the fountain seemed to come to life as Mr. Silk materialized in his pale suit, from where he had been standing beside them. He stepped down and tipped his hat to Johnny Fivetails.

The coyote feral reached out and shook hands with Mr. Silk.

"You're late," said the moth feral. "He cannot abide tardiness."

Johnny shrugged. "I came as soon as his creature got to me," he said.

"No matter," said Mr. Silk, with a dismissive wave. "How are our *friends*?"

Caw's chest felt tight.

"Like putty in my hands," said Johnny. "I reckon the fox feral still has a thing for me. Sounds like her marriage is going down the drain."

Caw saw Lydia's fists clench tight on the branch.

"I'd like to say I see a romantic future for you there," said Mr. Silk, chuckling, "but I think that would be unlikely. You're sure no one suspects?"

Johnny laid a hand on Mr. Silk's shoulder. "Stop worrying," he said. "It's gone exactly how he said it would. They're all looking for the crow talker. They think he's a liability, and they're right. I can't see how the kid got the better of you before. He's nothing like his mother—she might have been naive, but at least she was tough."

Caw felt sick with anger. How had he fallen for the coyote feral's treacherous act?

"Trust me," said Mr. Silk. "I've seen him do things with those crows you wouldn't believe."

Johnny gave a dismissive snort. "Sure. I've heard it all before. So, where is everyone?"

Mr. Silk lifted a hand and a stream of moths rose in a swirling column. Caw's pulse quickened as a huge shape drifted through the trees to their left. An eagle alighted on the edge of the fountain. Then Lugmann paced into the clearing with a panther at his side.

"Fivetails," he said.

One by one, more of the enemy ferals emerged. Monkeys clambered over the stone nymphs, chattering excitedly. The dreadlocked centipede feral, who Caw hadn't seen since the battle against the Mother of Flies, came from behind a tree. His body appeared to squirm as his creatures threaded in and out of his clothes and hair. Then, riding on her bison's back, came the shaven-headed woman. Gradually, there came dogs, snakes, and huge bulbous toads. A mountain lion. Dozens of men and women and their beasts. The leaves in the trees shook with screeches until the scrapping animals were commanded to part.

They're all here, thought Caw. *The White Widow's army.*

Too many for me and Lydia to take on alone.

"Okay," said Johnny. "Let's put this plan into action."

Lugmann rubbed his hands together. "They won't know what's hit them."

Johnny headed off at a jog through the trees, toward the park gates.

"We need to warn the others," said Lydia.

"Go back the way we came in," Caw replied. "When you're out

of earshot, call your mom—tell her everything. That Johnny is working against us and that the convicts are here."

Whatever their enemies were planning, it had to be stopped.

"What about you?" said Lydia.

Caw gritted his teeth. *I'm going to settle a score,* he thought.

"Caw?"

He brandished the Crow's Beak, which gleamed darkly. Caw didn't want to hide anything from Lydia, but it was better if she didn't know what he was planning. "I'm staying here."

Lydia looked uncertain. "But you haven't got your crows. If you're found . . . Why don't you come with me—help me explain?"

Caw shook his head. "They don't trust me anymore," he said. "But they'll believe you. Say you came here looking for me but found Johnny instead. Please, Lydia—just go."

She bit her lip, hesitating. "Promise me you'll be careful," she said, then turned and ran off through the trees.

Caw waited until she was out of sight, then skirted around the edge of the gathering. Peering between hedgerows, he saw Johnny slip through the front gates of the park and jog into the street beyond. Silently, Caw went after him.

As he tailed the traitorous feral, Caw realized the extent of Johnny Fivetails's scheming. He had been playing the good ferals from the start, and now he knew all their secrets. Johnny had been at Pickwick's bank because it was part of the plan to convince them that he was on their side. It had been his idea to hit the sewing factory, and he'd engineered Caw's meeting with the White Widow. All to make Caw look bad and put himself in charge.

Caw watched Johnny's back with growing hatred. Whatever the coyote feral was planning now would fail. Caw wasn't going to be manipulated again.

Johnny Fivetails cut into an alley between an old printing works and the high wall of the prison. Caw waited a few moments, then followed, keeping to the shadows. The coyote feral was speeding up and Caw quickened his steps. The alley was a dead end.

A bloodcurdling animal cry from behind Caw made him jump. Johnny stopped in his tracks. Caw slipped behind a Dumpster so he couldn't be seen, then waited for the sound of Johnny's steps to continue. Instead he heard a low growl. Caw's neck hair pricked up, and he turned to see a coyote enter the alley. It padded slowly forward.

"What's that you've found, Victor?" asked Johnny, with amusement in his voice. "A cowering crow?"

There was no use hiding anymore. Caw stepped out. Johnny was grinning, twenty paces away. With his enemy in front and the coyote behind, Caw had nowhere to run.

"Now *where* have you been?" said Johnny. "We've been looking all over for you."

"I've been discovering the truth," said Caw. "About you."

Johnny spread his arms. "And what do you think you know about me?" he said.

"You're working for the Spinning Man. You've betrayed everyone who trusted you."

The coyote's throat rumbled. It lowered its head and showed its teeth.

"We both made our choices," said Johnny. His eyes flicked up to the surrounding rooftops, and Caw realized he was looking for crows. "I chose to side with the winners."

"Just like that?" said Caw. "But in the Dark Summer you fought *against* the spider feral."

"I sided with the winners then, as well," said Johnny. "Honor, loyalty, courage—they're just words, Caw. Words winners use to create their lies. *Survival* is the only word that matters. It's a shame you've only just learned that. Black Corvus knew it well."

"He was a monster," said Caw. "I'm nothing like him."

"I know," said Johnny. "That's why it ends here for you."

"I don't think so," said Caw. "I can call a thousand crows to fight you."

Johnny looked around again. With every second that passed, fear gripped Caw harder. Johnny smiled. "Interesting. Where are they, then, Caw?"

"They'll be here," said Caw. "Don't force me to take you on."

Johnny laughed. "You're a terrible liar, Caw. Even if you could summon your crows, Victor will be on you in five seconds and you'll be dead in ten."

Caw glanced sideways. There was a drainpipe attached to the crumbling wall. If he could get to it, perhaps he could climb out of reach and gain some kind of advantage.

"Cool your boots," said Johnny. "The White Widow ordered me not to kill you. It's a shame—I would have liked to fight you. See what all the fuss is about."

Caw gripped the Crow's Beak tightly. "You're coming with me," he said.

Johnny didn't look in the slightest bit troubled. In fact, there was a glint in his eye. "Of course, I could always claim self-defense. Unlike you, I have a certain gift for telling lies." He nodded beyond Caw. "He's yours, Vic."

The coyote sprang forward, eating up the alley in huge strides. "Wait!" said Caw, backing away. As the coyote launched itself into the air, Caw swung the Crow's Beak, bracing himself for impact.

15

Caw heard an earsplitting yowl as he fell, and several parts of his body erupted with pain. The coyote was lying on top of him, its neck and head hanging over his shoulder. His face was inches from its bared teeth. But its eyes were closed, and its flanks rose and fell rapidly. Then, with one last shuddering exhalation, the coyote went still.

Caw heaved it off, wriggling his legs from beneath its dead body. His jacket was covered in blood, and so was the blade of the Crow's Beak.

"Vic?" said a shaky voice. Caw saw Johnny Fivetails standing at the end of the alley, openmouthed. "What did you do to Victor?" he said.

Caw was shaken. "I didn't mean to," he said, lowering the sword.

Johnny snarled, "You little rat!" He charged and plowed into Caw's stomach, shoulder first. They both fell and sprawled on the ground. The Crow's Beak rattled away across the pavement. Caw felt a hand clawing his face, fingers scratching at his eyes. He clamped his teeth over Johnny's wrist and bit down hard.

"Ow!" yelled the coyote feral. He shoved Caw off, sending him crashing into a Dumpster. Johnny stood up, yanked his jacket straight, and inspected his bleeding wrist. "You'll pay for that," he said. He drew back a foot and kicked Caw in the gut.

Caw's breath went out of him, leaving a hollow of pain. He gasped, but managed to clamber up on one knee. Johnny backed up, then ran in again for another kick. Caw swung out a foot and tripped the coyote feral mid-swing. Johnny hit the ground with a thump.

Caw crawled toward the Crow's Beak, still struggling to draw a breath. He felt Johnny grab at his ankle but pulled free. His fingers found the hilt of the sword, and he whipped around to face his attacker.

Johnny raised both hands in surrender, breathing hard. Caw scrambled to his feet, keeping the blade steady and the point leveled at Johnny's heart.

"You haven't got it in you," sneered the coyote feral.

"Haven't I?" said Caw, firmly grasping the hilt of the Crow's Beak.

"Look, let's work together, Caw," said the coyote feral. "I know *all* his plans. What d'you say?"

"Tell me where Selina is," said Caw, "and I'll let you live."

Johnny shook his head. "You don't get it, do you? She's the White Widow. There's nothing—"

"Where is she?" said Caw again.

"She's probably dead already," said Johnny. "He only needed her until he was strong enough without a vessel. He's coming back, Caw. Nothing can stop him. And when he's here, it won't matter how many ferals Velma can scrape together for her little army."

Caw hated the look in Johnny's eyes. Not because it was malicious, but because it was so resigned. Like there was no hope for another future at all.

"Just tell me where I can find Selina," said Caw.

A slow smile spread across Johnny's face. "Don't worry, Caw— you'll see her soon enough." His eyes flicked over Caw's shoulder. *"In the Land of the Dead."*

Caw turned and saw three coyotes padding down the alley. Then he felt the Crow's Beak shoot from his grasp as Johnny struck, knocking the blade aside.

"Let's see how you do without a weapon," said Johnny as he backed away, grinning gleefully.

There was no way out. Behind Caw was the dead end of the alley. He could die cowering or fighting, but either road led to the same place.

He raised his fists.

Then, with a sudden flapping, two crows dropped from the sky and landed at his side. A plump male, feathers dull black and beak stubby, and a wiry female. Caw could hardly believe it.

Glum and Shimmer!

In that moment, he could have cried. "Thank you," he said, his voice barely a whisper. The crows just ruffled their feathers in response.

"Three against three." Johnny laughed. "Not exactly a fair fight, though."

The coyotes began to run with loping strides and the two crows took off, squawking. Caw was filled with a new energy. He lurched to one side, gripping the drainpipe in both hands, and began to climb.

"After him!" yelled the coyote feral.

The coyotes sprinted forward and the lead one pounced. Caw swung his body out of reach and heard the scrape of claws down the brick wall. Surging panic helped him scramble higher as the three creatures snapped and lunged below.

Johnny Fivetails grabbed another drainpipe farther along the building and began to climb with unnerving speed. But Caw was faster.

Years of scaling the roofs of Blackstone and the hundreds of trees he'd climbed gave Caw the edge. He reached the top of the building and rolled over the parapet onto the roof. His trailing leg caught on something and pain lanced through his calf. He winced and saw that a rusted prong of metal had ripped through his jeans and gashed his skin. Blood dripped into the alley below.

He unhooked the denim from the prong, peering over the parapet. Coyotes watched him with hungry stares.

Then a scrabbling much closer drew his attention, and he saw Johnny clambering onto the roof. Caw realized that they were on top of the old prison. He remembered that there was a series of exercise yards on the other side of this roof, enclosed by the outer walls.

Johnny peered over the edge. "Long drop, Caw," he said. "And look what I found."

He reached behind him and drew the Crow's Beak from his belt.

Glum and Shimmer circled and landed at Caw's side. Still loyal, despite everything. He backed away as Johnny Fivetails advanced with the blade.

Caw glanced over his shoulder and saw he was getting close to the edge by a prison yard. In the past, he would have used his feral powers to transform into a crow. But he had no doubt that Corvus had taken that option away from him too.

"Tell you what, Caw—here's a choice," said Johnny. "You can either jump or I run you through."

Caw tried to breathe steadily. Backward meant certain death— nothing Glum or Shimmer could do alone would save him. So he could only go forward. If he could somehow avoid the blade, he might have a chance. But Johnny Fivetails looked deadly. He wouldn't miss.

But perhaps there was another way.

"Wait!" said Caw. "I've got something for you."

"There's nothing you have that I want," said Johnny. "Stop stalling."

Caw reached up to his neck. "What about the Midnight Stone?" he said.

He heard the breath catch in the coyote feral's throat. "You're lying. You don't have it," he said.

Caw drew out the stone, still wrapped in its pouch.

Johnny's eyes gleamed and he licked his lips. "Give it to me," he said.

"And you'll let me live?" said Caw as he unlooped the cord from his neck.

Johnny shook his head. "Nice try."

Caw tossed the pouch backward over his shoulder.

"No!" said Johnny, lowering the blade as he watched the Midnight Stone plummet over the edge. It was all the distraction Caw needed. He dived forward, aiming to punch Johnny in the face. But the coyote feral grabbed his arm and they toppled over, landing in a heap on the roof. They rolled as one, and Caw had no idea how close they were to the edge. His hands found Johnny's throat and he squeezed. The coyote feral clenched his chin to his chest and broke Caw's grip. Then he lifted his head, and—*smack!*—drove his forehead into the bridge of Caw's nose.

Caw was paralyzed by pain. Johnny rolled him onto his back and pressed down with a great weight. Then there was a fist in Caw's ribs and another crunching into his cheekbone. He tasted blood in his mouth and heard the panicked cries of the crows.

Suddenly the weight lifted. Caw's face throbbed from the blows. He glanced across the rooftop and saw that Johnny Fivetails had snatched up the Crow's Beak again.

"That was childish, Caw," he said. "Childish and foolish. My coyotes are going to enjoy you as their next meal—"

Johnny was interrupted by a new voice. "Leave him be!"

Caw propped himself up on his elbows. There, standing on a peaked section of the roof, was a dark, portly figure, with a black creature crouched at his ankles. For a moment, Caw thought his eyes were deceiving him.

"*Felix Quaker,*" said Johnny. "I thought you were smart enough to stay out of this. That's normally your style, isn't it? Curl up in a ball somewhere and hope that no one bothers you?"

Caw wiped the blood away from his cheek. His head was still spinning.

Quaker picked his way to their level with surprising agility, his cat sticking close to his side. As they came into the light, Caw saw it was same cat he and Lydia had met on the park wall.

"Let's just say you persuaded me otherwise," said Quaker. Caw saw that Quaker's face was swollen and purple on one side. "Cats are slow to anger, but we can be fierce. You shouldn't have followed me, Johnny. You should have left me well alone." More cats appeared, fanning across the rooftop to surround Johnny.

"Sorry about the jaw," Johnny Fivetails smirked. "You weren't very helpful with my inquiries."

"Caw, are you hurt?" asked Quaker.

"I'm okay," said Caw weakly.

"Not for much longer," said Johnny. He spun without warning, raising the Crow's Beak high above Caw's head. But as he did so, Quaker's black cat pounced onto the coyote feral's arm. With a yowl, Johnny dropped the sword as he swung his arm wildly to throw the cat off.

"Come on, Quaker!" yelled Johnny. "Let's see how an angry tomcat fights!"

As Caw staggered to his feet, Quaker and Fivetails circled each other. The cat feral moved fast, hunched and low, his feet seeming to glide across the rooftop. Johnny Fivetails bounced on his toes, fists raised like a boxer.

"You know, maybe we're not so different after all," said Johnny. "We both like to sit on the fence before joining the fight."

The cat feral charged, hands a blur. Johnny sidestepped and

the older man barreled past. He skidded, just managing to stop at the edge of the roof that overlooked the street. Johnny ran at him, hands outstretched to shove Quaker to his death. But Felix spun around, bringing his arms up and grabbing hold of Johnny's wrists. For a moment they strained against each other on the precipice.

Then Quaker smiled. "I'm nothing like you, Fivetails," he said. "You'd sell your soul to the highest bidder. Well, not anymore."

And then he stepped back into thin air.

Johnny Fivetails screamed as they both went toppling over the edge.

"Felix!" cried Caw.

Gripped with horror, he crawled to the side of the roof. He didn't want to look, but he had to know. He leaned over, expecting to see two smashed bodies lying on the ground.

But three stories down there was only one. Johnny Fivetails lay on his back in the alley, one leg folded at an angle beneath the other, arms splayed out on either side.

Felix Quaker was crouching a few feet away from Johnny, on his hands and knees. He stood up stiffly and craned his neck to look at Caw.

It was forty feet down. Maybe more. Any normal person would be dead, for sure.

"How . . . ?"

"We always land on our paws," called Quaker from below.

Caw smiled, despite everything. Then he saw Johnny's arm twitch, and his chest expanded with a heaving groan. Quaker jumped back in surprise. "You'd better get down here," he said.

With his leg still bleeding and his face beginning to swell around his eyes, Caw picked his way carefully down another drain-pipe, hopped across the ledge of a barred window, then dangled and dropped the remaining way to the ground. Glum and Shimmer landed next to him, with the Crow's Beak grasped in their talons. Glum dipped his beak and the Midnight Stone rattled on the paving stones. Caw was overwhelmed to have his crows at his side once more. "You came back," he said. "I didn't call you, but you came."

The crows looked at him, their black eyes impossible to read.

Caw put the stone in his pocket and sheathed the sword before turning to the cat feral. "Did you know you'd survive the fall?" he asked.

"I . . . hoped," said Quaker. "To be honest, I haven't tried it for a fair few years." He patted his stomach. "Not really been in training."

"Thank you," said Caw. "You saved my life."

Quaker nodded briskly. "I'd say you look terrible, my boy, but it's all relative." They looked at Johnny Fivetail's body. He was still breathing in shallow pants, and his fingers twitched. Caw guessed that his back was broken along with his leg and many other bones. It was a horrible sight. A pair of desperate eyes latched on to Caw's.

"Don't try to move. We'll call you an ambulance," Caw said.

Johnny Fivetails coughed, then spat blood across the gravel, his lips curling into a vicious smile. "It's not me who'll need it," he snarled.

"Caw!" said Quaker sharply. "We've got a problem." Caw stood up and saw the three coyotes stalking toward them. Johnny Fivetails chuckled.

Caw looked around for an escape route. There was a fire escape, but they'd never reach it before the coyotes. The beasts wrinkled their snouts, and Caw saw their master's cruelty reflected in their glares.

"I'll enjoy this," said Johnny Fivetails. "I've kept them hungry for days."

"Call your crows and get us out of here!" said Quaker, pressing closer to Caw.

"I can't," said Caw. "I . . . I don't control them anymore."

"*What?*" said Quaker. "But . . ."

Caw wondered if he could use the Midnight Stone as a distraction again. But even if it worked for one coyote, the other two were more than enough to kill them. The three beasts were less than twenty feet away and closing. Glum and Shimmer squawked and fluttered to his side.

Caw could only think of one thing to do.

He knelt and slipped the Midnight Stone out of its pouch, right into Johnny's open palm.

"What are you . . . ," mumbled the coyote feral. Then his eyes rolled in panic as Caw squeezed his fingers tight over the stone. "No! You can't . . ."

Johnny's body convulsed and the coyotes lay down, ears pressed back, as though they were suddenly afraid. Caw held on, keeping the coyote feral's hand clamped around the Midnight Stone. Swirls of light glowed within its black surface. The lights throbbed in time with Johnny's trembling breaths. At last he let out a moan of despair, and they faded suddenly like a lightbulb filament shorting out.

"What did you do?" asked Quaker.

Johnny moaned again, a ragged sound that seemed torn from deep within his stomach. "You took them!" he said. "You took my creatures from me!"

Caw peeled Johnny's fingers from the Midnight Stone and stowed it safely in its pouch. "You gave me no choice," he said quietly. The coyotes were yawning and licking their teeth nervously.

Johnny stared at Caw with pure hatred. "It's not over," he croaked. "He'll still win."

Caw shook his head. "Not without an army, he won't. Lydia is fetching our allies now. They're heading to the park to round up the convicts."

He waited for the defeat to register in Johnny's eyes, but instead he began to laugh—choking, pain-racked, unsettling laughter. "You fool," he gasped. "Don't you . . . see? I . . . was going to bring . . . them to the park anyway. It's an ambush . . . kid! A spider's web . . ." He choked on a mouthful of blood. "A web . . . to catch you all!"

Caw swallowed, cold prickling across his skin.

"We need to go, my boy," said Quaker urgently as he gripped Caw's shoulder. The two crows took off, circling above their heads.

"What about him?" asked Caw, nodding to Fivetails.

"Leave him," said Quaker, and a sudden burst of animal and human cries cut through the night. Caw hesitated. The noises were coming from the park. A moment later, Caw heard the crack of gunfire too.

"Caw! Come on!" said Quaker as he tugged on Caw's arm. Johnny's breath was coming faster and faster in ragged pants; then suddenly he went still and his eyes rolled into the back of his head.

"There's nothing we can do for him now," said Quaker.

And then the cat feral dragged Caw away through the alley. Neither the coyotes, nor Johnny, made another sound.

Caw was still shaking as they took a side street and heard another cacophony of screams.

"Hurry, Caw!" said Quaker.

But Caw was already running, with Glum and Shimmer soaring overhead.

16

"Wait for me!" shouted Quaker.

Caw cast a quick glance back and saw that several dozen cats had already fallen in behind the cat feral. He ran on, toward the front of the park. The gates were open, the central chain broken, and Caw sprinted inside. The first thing he saw was a fox lying on its side on the grass, panting quickly. Blood matted its muzzle. Then a huge guttural roar from the darkness beyond it sent a shiver down Caw's spine.

"Look out!" gasped Quaker.

Caw ducked as a shape swooped down through the shadowy trees on his left. In the glare of a streetlamp he caught a flash of white feathers and the yellow gleam of a jagged beak. The eagle narrowly missed him, sailing in between the branches of another tree. Caw quickly followed the sounds of battle into the darkness at the heart of the park. Leaves rustled overhead, and he saw squirrels scurrying among the branches, under attack from a second eagle. *Madeleine's here too.*

A flock of pigeons whipped past overhead, carrying a screaming monkey. Through the trees, Caw saw Crumb partially hidden by a bench. The pigeon feral moved his arms frantically, as if conducting several orchestras at once. Behind him something was stalking through the grass. As it entered a pool of moonlight, Caw realized it was a huge monitor lizard, snapping its fearsome jaws.

"Crumb, look out!" yelled Caw.

The pigeon feral spun around, then jumped back as the lizard lunged at his leg. Pigeons fell across its back at once while others soared down and snatched Crumb away from danger. He flew toward Caw.

"Thank God you're all right," he said, hovering above. "We came as soon as we heard." He shook his head, scanning the trees with wide, anxious eyes until his gaze fell on Shimmer and Glum, perched on a branch nearby. "Is it true, Caw . . . about your crows?"

Caw was about to answer when the grass on his right started to move. Rats—hundreds of them, heading straight for him. They swarmed over the path.

"Help!" cried a young voice.

"Pip!" said Crumb, and his pigeons swept him off over the trees.

A wave of Quaker's felines met the rats in a screeching, hissing chaos, but many of the rodents broke through. Caw ran from the swarm, still heading toward the center of the park. He was panting hard, his limbs burning with adrenaline. He saw the bison feral and her huge beast standing on the smashed remains of a picnic table.

They looked frightened, surrounded by snarling, snapping wolves. Racklen was leaning against a tree nearby and clutching a bleeding arm. A man with torn clothes pulled out a gun and advanced on the wolf feral, but a second before he could pull the trigger, his face was coated in bees. The shot ricocheted off into the night as he stumbled, his screams muffled by buzzing.

Caw moved on, desperately searching for Mrs. Strickham, Lydia, and Pip, but he could only see more dim, shadowy shapes. From above came the sound of snapping branches and Crumb tumbled out of a tree, landing heavily. Pigeons flocked around him, many with feathers hanging loose.

"Go!" he croaked. "Help Pip!"

Caw spotted his friend in the children's playground, running past the old carousel. Pip vaulted the fence and dived through a gap under the bandstand steps. Monkeys scrambled after Pip, pummeling him with their fists and ripping at his clothes. Mice covered the monkeys' backs, but the monkeys ignored them. Caw ran for the bandstand. He grabbed a monkey by the nape of its neck and tossed it away. Another bit his hand, but he shook that one free as well. He tried to kick another, but it ran up his body, clawing for his throat. Caw managed to seize its tail and hurled it away across the grass. At last the monkeys retreated, and Caw helped Pip to his feet as the mice disappeared inside the young boy's coat.

A ball of snarling feathers and fur streaked past. Two foxes, fighting with an eagle, slammed against the bottom of a tree, and Caw saw the eagle slice a fox's flank open with a razor-sharp talon, then lift the other into the sky, the fox squirming in its grip. The eagle only got to tree level before raccoons leaped from the branches. One missed, but the second landed on the eagle's back and they fell to the ground. Mrs. Strickham appeared from behind the tree, her long coat flapping as she ran to the injured fox, while the eagle broke free and took off with heavy wing beats.

Caw ran to her.

"Johnny Fivetails—" he began.

"Caw!" said Mrs. Strickham, looking up at him in shock. "Lydia told us everything. I'm so, so sorry for everything, Caw. I can't believe we—"

"He's dead," said Caw.

Mrs. Strickham's expression froze. Then she said quietly, "How?"

"He tried to kill me, but Quaker saved my life."

"Quaker?" said Mrs. Strickham. "*Felix* Quaker?"

Caw nodded.

The battle was still raging all around them. Caw saw the flock of parakeets swoop past, then dive toward something out of sight. A moment later, there was a shout of alarm.

"Lydia told us about your crows, Caw," said Mrs. Strickham. "We'll find a way to get them back."

Caw wished he could believe her. He looked around, but he couldn't see Glum or Shimmer anywhere. He hoped they were staying out of danger.

A fox hobbled toward them, limping on a broken leg. "Poor Tia," murmured Mrs. Strickham. The creature cocked its head and made a mewling sound.

Mrs. Strickham looked up quickly. "Where?" she said. The fox made another sound, and Mrs. Strickham began to run.

"Wait!" said Caw.

"It's Lydia!" Mrs. Strickham called back. "I *told* her not to come. . . ."

She had only made it as far as the next tree when the dreadlocked convict stepped into her path. Suddenly the ground seethed with hundreds of centipedes, flooding around her ankles. More dropped from the branches above her and squirmed under Mrs. Strickham's clothes, and she doubled over. Caw ran toward her.

"Caw, leave me!" yelled Mrs. Strickham. "Find Lydia!"

The convict leered at Caw as he darted past. But then a pack of foxes launched themselves at him. Up ahead, Caw saw pigeons pinning down the monkey feral and Racklen charging forward. A fierce-looking German shepherd was surrounded by cats, growling. Huge hares were locked in battle with rats by the fountain, and a wolf dragged a convict by his arm, with moths covering its body like a second layer of fur.

Glancing upward, Caw saw that Glum and Shimmer had returned. And with them were several dozen crows! With a rush of hope he tried to summon them, but he couldn't feel a thing. The crows were watching, stock-still, without emotion.

Then he spotted Lydia. She was in the shadow of a thick grove of trees, waving a branch back and forth as two panthers stalked in front of her. One leaped and snapped the branch in two with its jaws. Lugmann strolled behind his beasts, slowly and confidently.

Lydia swung her stub of branch, but it was nowhere near long enough to keep them at bay. She tripped over a tree root, landing with a thud on her back. Caw put on a burst of speed and leaped in front of her, slashing with the Crow's Beak at the two big cats. The panthers hesitated but didn't turn tail. Caw hauled Lydia up and they backed away from the snarling creatures. Lydia was bleeding—one of the panthers must have got hold of her arm before Caw reached her. She pressed her hand against the wound, gritting her teeth.

Lugmann placed a hand on each of his panthers' necks. "Your little blade isn't going to help you now," he said, eyes glinting in the dark.

Caw collided with a tree trunk behind him. Nowhere else to run. The panthers wrinkled their muzzles and snarled.

In the tree nearby, the crows still watched. *Please,* said Caw. But they didn't move.

"Any last words?" said Lugmann. "I can't promise it will be quick."

"Go to hell," said Lydia.

Lugmann smiled. "One day, perhaps." His glare turned cold and pitiless, and he lifted his hands. "Kill them," he said.

The panthers froze.

The convict frowned and gave one of his beasts a vicious kick in the flank. "Tear them to pieces!" he snapped.

The big cat pawed the ground and the other lay down, purring.

Caw exchanged a glance with Lydia. *Why aren't they attacking?*

Lugmann's eyes widened as he gazed upward, and he stepped back. "Come on," he commanded, turning and walking away quickly.

Caw tilted his head and saw that the tree trunk above them was *moving.*

The bark was rippling and bristling.

All the leaves were black and heavy, drooping with the weight of small creatures.

On lengths of silken thread they began to drop to the ground, while others surged along the branches toward the trunk.

Spiders.

Caw grabbed Lydia's hand and tugged her away, crunching spiders beneath his feet. As he looked back, he saw the White Widow crouched among the canopy, white hair hanging over her face, eyes glistening black.

In a rush of dizzy recognition, Caw realized it was *his* tree.

The one where his nest had once been.

His *home* for nearly ten years.

She must have known.

The White Widow's head twitched sideways and she dropped to the ground, landing on all fours in the grass.

She didn't stand, and Caw's heart lurched with a mixture of fear and pity. Selina's face was skeletal, her cheekbones bladelike, with dark patches of what looked like rotting skin. Her nails were at least two inches long, black and pointed as they dug into the earth. Her hair, still white, had thinned so much he could see her scalp under the matted strands.

"Hello, Jack," she hissed, her tongue flickering between discolored teeth. "I thought I'd find you here."

Her head twitched again. Whether through starvation or simply the corruption of the Spinning Man's spirit, her skeleton seemed to have changed. Her legs, tucked up beneath her, looked stiff, and her elbows were oddly disjointed, splaying out the wrong way. Her spine curved unnaturally and her head sat low between her shoulders. She looked like some hideous hybrid of human and spider.

"Selina . . . ," said Lydia.

The White Widow laughed. "Not anymore," she said. "Your friend is dead, but this body has proved useful. I'm ready, Jack— ready to live again."

Caw's chest felt hollow. Johnny Fivetails had been telling the truth about one thing.

It really was over. His friend was gone.

Lydia snatched the Crow's Beak from Caw's hand and lunged forward. With incredible speed, the White Widow scurried backward up the tree trunk and kicked out with a leg. It caught Lydia on the chin with a sickening thud. Her knees buckled and she collapsed.

"No!" shouted Caw. He ran to Lydia, but spiders swarmed toward him. By the time he reached her, they had covered his legs and were crawling up his waist. He scooped Lydia up in his arms and staggered away, but the spiders kept coming. He felt bites piercing his trousers and stinging his legs and then his stomach and his neck. He felt their legs scurrying under his hair and clothes. If he could just get Lydia back to her mother . . .

With every step, she felt heavier, and now Caw's legs wouldn't do what he told them. The spiders were still biting, and a strange feeling of weightlessness coursed through his blood. Each beat of his heart seemed to drive the poison further into his veins, separating him from himself, splitting mind from body. He stumbled and fell, dropping Lydia onto the grass. And when he tried to move, Caw couldn't stand.

Spiders rummaged beneath him and the ground began to move. They were carrying him—he was drifting on a sea of spiders. He could hear squawks and roars, grunts and angry cries as the other ferals fought. But slowly those sounds were drowned out by the rustling of the spiders' legs.

Then the rustling sounds vanished too and blackness closed in, swallowing him whole.

His first thought was of Lydia.

Where is she?

Caw was suspended in a white world. He tried to move, but his limbs felt too heavy. No, not heavy. *Stuck.* He was upright and swaths of silk lay in drapes in every direction. He made out dim shapes around him, and through the skeins of webbing, he recognized his surroundings. Somehow he was in his old house, his parents' bedroom.

He tore his wrist free and wriggled his body furiously. The cobwebs gave up their grip and he tumbled to the floor. Layers of silk still clung to him, smothering his face, and he tore them off, staggering to his feet. He methodically pulled away at the strands until he stood in a heap of broken webs, panting heavily. The air was warm and humid, suffused with a smell like rotting vegetation.

Webs stretched from floor to ceiling, wall to wall, but he saw no spiders. How long had he been unconscious? Was the battle at the park still going on? He remembered Selina—what she had become—and a bolt of grief hit him afresh.

Something moved behind the curtains of silk. Quickly, scurrying, through the door.

"Who's there?" he called.

"Come and find me," taunted the voice of the White Widow.

Caw shuddered. He looked around and was astonished to see the Crow's Beak lying on the floor. He wondered why she'd let him keep it.

Hacking with his sword, Caw cut a path through the webs. They clung to the blade in sticky strands as he forged a path to the door. On the landing outside, the webs were less dense, hanging between the rails of the banister and clustered into corners.

"Down here," hissed a voice. "I'm waiting for you."

Caw broke through the last of the webs and descended the stairs. He felt as though he was walking into a cave: spiders scuttled by his feet, huddling aside as if making way for him.

The ground floor was adorned in spiders' webs, casting everything in an eerie white glow. The webs twitched and he caught a glimpse of the White Widow moving quickly up a wall in the dining room. She moved in jerks, her arms and legs almost a blur. She stopped for a moment, hanging upside down from the ceiling, defying gravity. Then she scurried down the far wall and came to rest beside the fireplace. Her head rotated toward him.

"Home sweet home," she said, her voice a deathly rattle. "Do you like what I've done with the place?"

"What are we doing *here*?" said Caw.

"Why not here?" said the White Widow. "This is where it was always meant to end, the night I came for you."

The pain of Caw's earliest memory flashed brightly in his heart. The Spinning Man had killed his parents in this very room. He would have killed Caw too, if Elizabeth Carmichael hadn't pushed her only son from the upstairs window, entrusting him to the crows. The White Widow raised a fist and Caw saw the white spider running across her knuckles.

"He tells me you've tasted the truth," she said. "How was it?"

"What do you want?" retorted Caw.

"To make you realize how worthless you are," said the White Widow. "To make you pay for the crimes of the crows. To take *everything from you*." She used a long nail to scratch her face thoughtfully. "Your allies, your home, your powers—you've lost them all. Your friends in the park are dying as we speak."

Caw swallowed. "And Lydia?"

The White Widow laughed, a hollow, cold sound . . . but suddenly it became a choking scream. The spider feral collapsed onto the carpet, jerking and retching. Her bloodshot eyes bulged. Then with a groan, a swirl of white smoke spewed out of her lips.

The creature writhed in front of Caw, legs twitching. The smoke began to coalesce into a shape at her side. She turned to him, and in her straining, agonized face, Caw saw a glimpse of his old friend. Then, with a final heave, she collapsed.

"Selina!" he cried.

When a voice spoke again, it came not from the girl, but from the smoke.

A man's voice.

His voice.

And with each syllable, Selina moaned as if the words themselves added to her pain.

"*I take her life and live again,*" intoned the Spinning Man.

The white swirls billowed away from Selina's body, forming a ghostlike figure. With every second it grew more solid, until the last tendrils of smoke drifted from Selina's open lips.

All around the room, the spiders crowded closer, as though they were drawing power from their master's return. Caw felt his own strength leave him, and he fell at Selina's side, the Crow's Beak hanging limply in his hand. He tried to cradle her head—but it was a dead weight. Her eyes were open and vacant. She wasn't breathing.

"Selina . . . ," he said, his fingers searching for a pulse.

Nothing.

"It is done," said the Spinning Man.

Caw turned to see his enemy, horribly real once more. Horribly *alive*. It was the first time he'd ever seen the tall, black figure in the real world, and his body seemed to suck in the light from the room. The Spinning Man's face was as white as snow, his eyes solid black, like wells of oil.

Filled with a sudden surge of rage, Caw dived at him. He swung the Crow's Beak, but the Spinning Man caught Caw by the wrist. His nails were sharp black talons. Immediately Caw's hand went numb and a cold stab of pain spread up his arm. The Spinning Man smiled, revealing teeth filed to points. He rose above Caw, pushing the boy to his knees. "Look at me, Jack. Look me in the eyes!"

The Spinning Man reached across and plucked the sword, almost gently, from Caw's grasp. Caw knew in that instant what was coming next.

"No!" he cried.

The blade stabbed down in a flash, and Caw felt it bite deep into his shoulder, then pain like nothing he'd ever experienced exploded down one side of him. He stared in horror at the black metal piercing his clothing and his flesh. He could feel agony searing through his muscles. He tried to breathe, but the air wouldn't come. An iciness began to flood across his body.

"You're dying, Jack," said the Spinning Man. "Just like your wretched mother."

Caw tried to stand, but the pain was too great.

The Spinning Man's face drew closer, and Caw saw his own reflection in the black orbs of his enemy's eyes. At last, the Spinning Man tugged the Crow's Beak free, spattering the carpet with blood. Caw collapsed to the ground.

Darkness crowded the edges of Caw's vision. The Spinning Man dropped the Crow's Beak on the carpet and Caw reached out, desperately fumbling for the hilt. But though he closed his fingers around it, he couldn't lift the blade. His strength was ebbing away, the pain beginning to subside as he lost his grip on consciousness. He tried to fight, to stay awake, but all the warmth had evaporated from his limbs. His eyes longed to close, to welcome death. He fought to suck air into his lungs. His eyelids fluttered open and he saw the Crow's Beak, red with his blood. *Breathe.* The legs of the Spinning Man. *Breathe.* The empty fireplace. *Breathe.* Selina's dead face. *Breathe!*

If only he could reach out. If only he could touch her . . .

Then there were no more breaths to take.

17

White light, brighter than bright, utterly blinding.

Overwhelming cold, deep in his bones.

Caw blinked and blinked, trying to see.

He still couldn't breathe.

He couldn't feel anything at all.

But he tasted something—crystals of ice on his tongue. Then he lifted his head and saw a carpet of whiteness stretching all the way to the horizon.

Snow?

Caw flexed his fingers, pushing himself up. He was still holding the Crow's Beak. He knelt in the snow as flakes spun around him in the eddies of a gusting breeze. He looked down at his body. There were no wounds—his clothes weren't even ripped.

For a split second, Caw felt a surge of relief. Then crushing panic, because he knew this place and what it meant.

Caw was in *the Land of the Dead.*

He had been here once before, but not like this. Not when he was actually—

223

"Caw!" called a distant, wind-smothered voice.

He turned in the direction of the voice, sliding the blade into its sheath. About fifty yards away was a forest, the branches drooping with the weight of snow. Someone was watching him from among the trees. He squinted through the spinning snow. It was a girl with black hair and black clothes. She reached out and her voice carried on the breeze.

"Caw!"

It was Selina.

Caw struggled toward her, sinking up to his knees in snow with every step as his breath burned in his chest. He tried to ignore what it meant that they were both here, in this land.

By the time he reached the trees, Selina was gone.

He peered into the forest and saw another movement, several yards away. "Selina, come back!" he shouted.

"I'm trying," she called out, sounding desperate and afraid. "Caw, what is this place?"

He crunched across the ground, but each time he reached the point where she'd been standing, Selina slipped farther into the forest's depths.

"Selina!" he cried as she vanished out of sight.

Caw strode on. Above him the branches creaked eerily, and his breath formed clouds in the air. The snow glowed almost blue in the light of dusk. At last he saw Selina once more. She was standing in the middle of a snow-carpeted clearing, hugging herself and shivering. She looked so . . . alive—just a normal girl.

"Caw, where are we?" she said.

Caw paused, worried that if he moved closer she would simply vanish again. "It's all right," he said, trying to sound confident. "I'm with you now."

She smiled thinly. "You didn't answer my question. What is this place?"

He couldn't hide the truth from her. "This is the Land of the Dead," he said.

Her smile vanished. "You mean we're . . . both of us . . ."

Caw nodded. "I'm sorry, Selina. I tried to save you."

He took a step toward her, and this time she didn't move. "I saw it all, Caw," she said, her voice little more than a whisper. "I *felt* it all, but I couldn't stop him. I was losing myself, bit by bit." Her lips trembled and she sniffed, looking at the ground. "There was nothing I could do."

"It's not your fault," said Caw.

"No . . . it's yours!" called a voice.

Selina gasped and Caw spun around. On the other side of the clearing stood a figure dressed entirely in black.

For a moment Caw thought it was the Spinning Man.

But no. It was Black Corvus.

"Jack," he said. His eyes glittered coldly.

Selina stepped back, nearer to Caw.

Caw saw clumps of snow falling from the trees opposite. White crows had emerged from the pale sky and settled on the branches. There were hundreds of them.

But none landed on the branches above Caw. It was as if they had stopped at an invisible barrier right above Black Corvus.

Help us, Caw willed.

The crows stared at him with a cold malice, and Caw painfully remembered that these were not his crows anymore.

"Who's that?" asked Selina.

"Yes, do introduce us," said Black Corvus.

Caw shouldn't have been surprised to find his ancestor here. Quaker had once told him that all spirits lingered for a time in the Land of the Dead. Most faded away eventually, but those with a strong connection to the living world could sometimes cling on forever.

"This is Black Corvus," said Caw. "He's a murderer, a liar, and a coward."

"Oh, great," muttered Selina.

"And the most powerful feral who ever lived," said Corvus.

"Even better," said Selina.

"And with the help of the Crow's Beak, I will live again," said Corvus. "Give it to me, Jack."

Caw's hand dropped to his sword. And then he remembered— how he had escaped this place before. He unsheathed the Crow's Beak. "Come closer," he whispered to Selina.

Selina eyed the blade nervously. "What are you going to do?"

Caw held the sword in front of him, then took a deep breath. With a deliberate swipe, he sliced at the air in front of them.

There was no resistance. No flash of light. No tear in the fabric of the snow-filled air. Caw tried again, with the same effect.

"Only the crow talker can wield the Crow's Beak," said Corvus. "Hand it over, boy."

"Never," Caw replied.

Black Corvus's face darkened with anger. Above him, the white crows ruffled their feathers.

"I'm the only one who can face the Spinning Man, Jack—you know that. You've failed already."

"I beat him before," said Caw.

Corvus shook his head. "No, you let him back in. And look what that has achieved."

"Don't give it to him," said Selina.

"Keep out of this, girl," said Corvus. His mouth twisted as he lifted his hands. "This is your last chance, Caw."

Caw did not reply.

"Very well," said Corvus.

He dropped his hands and the crows took off from the branches, sweeping toward Caw like white darts. Caw shoved Selina aside, and she landed with a thump.

Then the crows hit him.

Caw was slammed into the snow, and he dropped the Crow's Beak. He tried to cover his face as hundreds of birds tore at his skin with their beaks. Caw tried to roll, but they kept on landing across his body. He cried out "Stop!" but he could hardly hear his own voice above the shrieks of the angry birds.

Then their weight was gone as they lifted away in a single mass.

Caw rolled over, plunging his bleeding hands into the snow to numb the pain. Selina knelt at his side.

"Are you okay?" she said.

Caw shook his head. As he had rolled, he had seen that Black Corvus was holding the Crow's Beak.

The crows were settling on the branches once more. Corvus smiled as he inspected the blade. "It's been too long," he said.

Caw staggered to his feet. He couldn't let it happen. He had to stop Black Corvus.

Somehow.

In his desperation, Caw found strength. He ran at Black

Corvus, kicking up the snow with clumsy strides. Corvus grinned, sidestepped nimbly, and slashed with the blade. Caw fell headlong as his blood spattered on the snow. A split second later he felt pain sear through his leg. A deep gash shone red above his knee.

"Stop wasting my time!" shouted Corvus, wiping the blade against his sleeve. "You're just a boy. A *weakling*!"

Caw tried to stand, but Corvus planted a foot on his chest, knocking him back into the snow. As he lay there, Caw saw the murder of white crows looking down. *Pitiless.* But, for some reason, his eyes were drawn to one in particular. It was the way it perched, the angle of its head.

"Screech?" he whispered.

The crow blinked.

"They're not listening," said Corvus. "You have to bend them to your will. You have to *show* them your power. If they don't fear you, no one will."

"I don't want them to fear me," said Caw, pushing himself up. "I don't want to be a murderer like you!"

Caw noticed that Selina was moving closer. One of the crows made a clicking sound and Corvus spun to face the girl. "Keep your distance," he commanded as he stabbed the air with the sword. Selina backed off.

Then Corvus raised the sword in both hands and brought

it down in an arc. There was a sudden flash of light, and a tear opened in midair, revealing a black void.

A passage back to the Land of the Living.

Caw felt the crows' eyes on him. Hundreds of them.

Please, he begged. *In the name of all crows, don't let this happen.* Caw looked again for the one he'd thought was Screech but couldn't see him. His whole body was freezing. He tried to stand, but fell forward as his leg gave way. His hands left bloody prints in the snow. As Corvus began to walk toward the opening, Caw gripped his ankle.

"Still fighting, boy?" said Corvus, looking down. "Why?"

Selina seized her chance, smashing into Black Corvus. He stumbled back from the black portal and fell down with a shout of rage. But he was up again in a flash, dusting the snow off his clothes, anger burning in his eyes.

He nodded to the sky. "Finish him."

The birds began to stretch their wings, but a sudden eerily wild crow squawk stilled them. The birds turned their heads together as a single bird landed in the center of the clearing next to Selina.

Even with the crow's feathers a ghostly white, Caw knew it was Screech.

"I told you to kill him," Black Corvus growled at the crows.

Again, the crows stirred, as if ruffled by the breeze. But only one took off, sailing over Caw's head. And instead of attacking the boy, it landed alongside Screech. Caw swallowed.

It was Milky, the white-feathered, blind crow he'd grown up with. There was no mistaking the wisdom of his stony stare.

Caw felt a rush of warmth in his blood. He looked at the crows, then at Black Corvus, who was frowning. "They're not listening to you, Corvus," he said. A strange power was building in the pit of Caw's stomach, like a fire taking hold. As his eyes swept over the snow-white crows, it grew, as if each bird were adding wood to the flames.

Corvus breathed sharply through his nose. He pointed the Crow's Beak into the trees. "Kill the boy! Kill them both—now!"

Selina reached down and Caw grasped her hand. Her fingers wrapped around his and her strength surged through him too. The crows remained where they were.

"Fine, I'll do it myself," snarled Black Corvus.

Caw saw his fearsome ancestor approaching, brandishing the Crow's Beak. He stood up, using his body to shield Selina.

Black Corvus lunged with the sword. Without thinking, Caw gripped it between his hands. As Corvus bore down with his weight, Caw resisted and the blade cut into his palms.

"That's the spirit!" said Corvus, gritting his teeth. "A shame it's come much too late."

The blade sliced through Caw's hands as it pressed closer to his chest. Pain screamed through his body. With every last drop of strength, he begged the crows to come.

Silently, the white flock swooped down from the branches. The air pressure seemed to subtly change. Corvus suddenly swallowed and staggered back. "What the . . . ?" he mumbled.

The first white crow thumped into his shoulder. Then two more swooped low, talons outstretched as they dug into his thigh. Black Corvus cried out in surprise. Another swept past his face and he flung his hands up with a yell, dropping the Crow's Beak. Caw saw blood rushing through his ancestor's fingers. Corvus stumbled blindly toward the trees as countless crows dive-bombed him, smashing into his body. He fell over and began to crawl, but the crows knocked him flat. Several landed on his body, scratching and stabbing. Black Corvus curled into a ball as they tore at his clothes. Caw saw more blood seeping through the ripped leather of Corvus's gloves as he tried to bat his attackers away.

"Stop!" Caw cried.

But the crows couldn't hear. Or if they could, they weren't listening.

Black Corvus's cries turned to moans, and his attempts to protect himself became weaker. Then he wasn't fighting at all. At last, the crows settled on the branches once more. The snow around Corvus's motionless body was stained red. And the dark portal shimmering in the air had vanished.

Caw saw that only two birds had remained outside the fray. *Screech and Milky.* They stared at Caw.

"You saved me," he said.

Screech hopped forward. Opened his beak.

You saved yourself, he said.

Caw's knees felt weak, but his heart was dancing. "I can understand you!" he cried.

The crows chose the one who is worthy, said Screech. *The one who fights not for himself but for the good of many.*

The pain in Caw's hands and leg was nothing as a smile spread across his face. "I thought I'd never be able to speak to you again. That I'd lost you all."

You will never lose us, said Screech. *We are bound to you.*

He looked older, wiser.

"White suits you," said Caw.

Go, Caw, said Screech. *They need you.*

Caw nodded. "Are you coming too?"

Screech looked at Milky, and the old crow's gaze was stern.

I cannot, said Screech, and Caw caught a trace of sadness in his voice. *My place is here.*

Caw couldn't leave Screech here, not like this. Not after all that his brave crow had done. Tears sprang into his eyes.

"Please, come with me," he said. "I need you, Screech. More than ever."

Leave, crow talker, said Milky. *This place is not for you. Not yet.*

Good-bye, Caw, said Screech, and Caw knew that the crow would never again return to the Land of the Living.

And so he turned his back on Screech and Milky and picked up the Crow's Beak from the snow. Its power flooded into his fingers at once. With a single flick, the point of the blade ripped open a black gash in the fabric of this world.

"Come on," he said to Selina, who had been quietly standing to one side. "It's time to go home." She shuffled toward the edge of the portal.

Then she hesitated and glanced back. "You are coming too, aren't you?" she said.

Caw lowered his head. Many crows had hopped onto Black Corvus's back, gripping his tattered clothing in their talons. Corvus's body rose from the ground, hanging limply beneath them, and Caw watched them carry it over the trees. The crows flew in convoy—a white cloud gradually blending with the white sky, until there was nothing left of them or Corvus to be seen. Somewhere among them were Screech and Milky.

The black hole ahead seemed to be leaking heat, as if Caw and Selina were standing near a fire.

"Caw?" said Selina.

He looked into the trees, and for a few moments he imagined

what it would be like to stay. A limbo existence without cares, or worries, or fear. An escape from Blackstone and the wars between the ferals. *Peace.* He'd earned it. He'd lost enough, hadn't he?

Then he felt Selina slip her warm hand into his.

Milky was right.

Not yet.

Caw turned and together they walked through the black doorway.

He was lying on the floor next to the fireplace, Selina prostrate beside him. The color had returned to her cheeks, and her black hair shifted as it hung across her face. She was breathing!

Spiderwebs hung above them, and through the strands of webbing, Caw saw movement on the other side of the room. His heart froze, a scream lodged in his throat.

Where the Spinning Man had stood before, there was a bulbous white abdomen covered in scraps of black clothing. A spider's legs had sprouted beneath it, white and almost translucent, and covered in fine hairs like the bristles of frost on winter branches.

Bile rose into Caw's throat.

The Spinning Man's head was distorted almost beyond recognition. Caw couldn't see his face, but the hair was white and hanging in ragged clumps. Beneath it, his scalp seemed slick with a sort of pale slime. His torso had shriveled, the skin wrinkled and blotchy, and his arms had shrunk into twitching limbs that ended in pale claws. His six other legs were like splinters of ice.

Caw stood up quietly, grasping the Crow's Beak. Despite the terror that threatened to paralyze him, his body felt stronger than ever before. The mortal wound in his shoulder had somehow healed, leaving only a dull ache. There was no trace of the cuts suffered in the Land of the Dead. But if the Spinning Man realized they were still alive, he would kill them in an instant. He needed to lead this spider creature away from Selina.

He needed the crows.

Caw edged around the table, ducking under strands of silk that crossed the room and stepping over others. If he could just get closer . . .

The Spinning Man's disgusting head rotated to face Caw. The only thing that remained of the once human face was the pale skin. His skull was squashed, the features flattened to pit-like nostrils, protruding black eyeballs, and a gaping, toothless maw.

"*It's not possible,*" said the monster's rasping voice. "*You were dead.*"

Caw filled his chest and straightened. "So were you," he replied.

And there, somewhere in the ether, he felt the flapping essence of the crows. *Come to me. . . .*

The Spinning Man's body turned, leg-points thumping on the floorboards.

"I don't know what's happened to you," said Caw. "But I'm not frightened."

The Spinning Man's mouth split in a grin and a thick black tongue flickered out. "*You should be,*" he hissed. "*My human body was always so frail. So I have chosen a new form. A greater form.*" He gestured to himself with a claw. "*I am no longer the spider feral, Jack Carmichael. I am the spider god.*"

He rushed at Caw, legs scrabbling, tearing through the webs.

Caw picked up a chair and hurled it across the room at the oncoming creature. The Spinning Man dodged easily, scurrying up the wall until he was right above Caw. As the hideous creature dropped, Caw dived across the floor. The Spinning Man landed with an ominous thud, crouching on his jointed spider knees.

"*No use running,*" he hissed.

Through the window, Caw saw something flash past—a dark winged shape.

The Spinning Man shot forward, barging straight into him. Caw fell backward over the sofa and onto the floor. The Spinning Man loomed across the top of the sofa, legs ready to stab. Caw rolled sideways as the first claw slammed down, then kicked out. His foot ached with the impact, like he had just kicked a tree trunk.

237

Caw scrambled backward, but the Spinning Man pursued him on scuttling legs. "After you're dead, the crow line will be finished. My spiders will hunt down your wretched birds and slaughter every single one."

Caw reached the bottom of the stairs. "You'll have to catch me first!" he yelled.

Then he turned and ran up the stairs, pushing his legs with all the strength he had. He was halfway up before the Spinning Man caught him. Caw turned and swung the Crow's Beak, and the blade lodged deep in one of the spider's legs. The Spinning Man leaped to the ceiling and the blade was torn from Caw's hand. He turned his head and hissed, his black tongue flapping in and out like a writhing snake. Then he reached down with a foreclaw, yanked the Crow's Beak free, and tossed it aside. Spots of black blood spattered onto the stairs like tar.

Caw vaulted over the banister and launched himself toward his bedroom. As soon as he was through the door, he tried to slam it closed, but it hit something solid. A monstrous spider leg scrabbled through the gap. Caw rammed his shoulder into the door and the leg retreated. He pushed the bolt across, breathing hard.

The wood of the door thundered under a heavy impact.

"*Let me in, let me in,*" taunted the Spinning Man in a singsong voice.

Caw ran to the window and flung it open. The cool night air

enveloped him. He felt a wave of unexpected dizziness as he looked at the drop below.

The door rocked on its hinges as the Spinning Man threw his weight against it.

Caw felt shaken as he stared out, as his past came rushing back to him. He'd been here before, held over the abyss. *As a child. In his dreams.* The night his mother and father had pushed him out.

It was happening all over again.

The wood of the door splintered, but the lock still held. The tip of a spider leg pushed through the crack.

Caw looked up at the starlit sky. His crows were out there, somewhere. He strained his eyes and his mind, begging them to come.

More panels of the door broke away and he saw the Spinning Man's vile face at the opening. It glistened with sweat, eyes mad with rage. "Open up, Jack," he said. "Don't run away from me!"

The sky was still empty.

The Spinning Man reached another claw through, feeling for the lock. He drew back the bolt, then pushed the remains of the door open. The gigantic spider squeezed into the room. With his back to the open window, Caw faced his enemy. There was something out there behind him, something building. He sensed flapping wings and open beaks devouring the night.

"*Here we are again,*" said the Spinning Man, stalking closer. He gazed around with mild curiosity. *"You know, I came for you that night too, as your parents lay dying downstairs. But they'd hidden you already."*

Caw's heart swelled with the sudden nearness of his crows.

They were here. They had come.

"Do your worst," he said.

"You cannot even imagine," said his enemy.

The Spinning Man ran across the carpet and Caw ducked as a black torrent swept in through the open window. The room seemed to fill with crows in less than a second, the air dense with feathers and fierce cries. Caw lost sight of the Spinning Man, then saw him scuttling this way and that, smashing into the walls as he sought to escape the onslaught. The crows swirled around him, taking turns to swoop in, attack, then climb away. The assault was relentless. The Spinning Man shrieked as his legs buckled beneath him like a spider caught in swirling water.

Caw saw with a hundred crows' eyes. He felt the power of their bodies. With just one thought, the murder swept away from the huge spider, then rammed him from the side, throwing him onto his back. Caw drove the beaks and talons into his enemy's soft underbelly. The spider legs writhed, but they couldn't stop the crows. He caught flashes of the Spinning Man through the consciousness of the birds—a thousand snapshots of hate-filled malice.

There was only one thing left to do.

Caw pressed the crows harder and they smothered every inch of the Spinning Man, gripping whatever they could in their talons. As one, they hoisted him into the air. Caw felt the weight of the monstrous spider. Heavy, yet light in the grasp of so many. They carried it in a ball of flapping black feathers, toward the open window.

The change happened almost without Caw noticing. Suddenly he was a crow.

He threw himself into the melee. Among the triumphant cacophony of cries, they carried the giant spider out into the night, climbing higher and higher.

Caw felt no mercy.

The pain of his parents, of Screech, the pain of all the Spinning Man's victims pressed on his heart and made it as black as the inky feathers of his crows.

They rose through the sky until Caw was higher than he had ever been before—Blackstone was just an illuminated sprawl in the midst of a vast land.

"I'll kill you, crow talker!" screeched the Spinning Man.

It is time, Caw told the crows.

Then he opened his talons, along with a hundred other crows.

For an instant, time seemed to freeze and the Spinning Man's eight-legged body hung in equilibrium.

Then he fell.

As the giant spider plummeted, splinters of white light ripped across its body. Caw watched as the shards of brightness tore it apart and heard its wretched scream sear through the night.

And long before the Spinning Man reached the ground, there was nothing of him left.

18

Caw felt suddenly weak, his wings sapped of power. They folded against his side and he began to drop through the currents of air, face upward, wind rushing through his feathers. Then the feathers were gone and he could feel his clothes flapping against his skin. He was a boy again, gravity dragging him earthward.

But he wasn't scared. As he fell, a feeling of serenity enfolded him. He saw the crows swooping from above and landing gently across his body, and with each that latched on, his descent slowed and weightlessness cushioned him. He gazed at the stars overhead as his crows carried him lower. He could sense in every wing beat their love for him.

At last they bore him through his bedroom window before laying him softly on the carpet and then flapping away through the open window. Only Glum and Shimmer remained, perching by Caw's side.

He's dead, said Glum, his voice wondrous to hear. *It's over.*

We did it, said Shimmer. *For Screech.*

Caw nodded, still lying faceup, swallowing back tears. He would tell them later what he had seen in the Land of the Dead. And he would never, ever forget it. "For Screech," he said.

After a few moments, he got to his feet and went to the window. Crows had alighted across the trees and turned to look at him, beady eyes glinting in the dark.

"Thank you," he said.

The birds warbled softly at first, but their voices rose to proud cries, filling the air and shaking the leaves with his name.

Caw! Caw! Caw!

After they fell silent, he heard a human voice from behind him. "Caw?"

Selina was standing in the doorway. Her hair was black and shining, her skin glowing. She looked stronger than ever.

"You're—you're fine," he said.

Then she grinned and ran into his open arms.

"He's gone," said Caw as she gripped him so tightly he thought his ribs might break. "Forever."

Selina broke away and glanced up, still smiling. "Thank you," she said.

Ahem . . . , said Glum. *That's quite enough of that.*

Caw broke the embrace. "We should get back to the park," he said. "They might need our help. Are you all right to fly?"

"As long as you don't drop me," said Selina. "I've already died once today."

And Caw laughed for what felt like the first time in years.

The crows carried them over the northern reaches of the city. Caw was battered and bruised, but he felt more at one with his crows than ever. They trusted him and he trusted them, completely and without question. Whatever had happened in the Land of the Dead—whatever bond had been re-formed there—it held in the Land of the Living too.

On the way to Blackstone Park, Selina told him everything. About Johnny Fivetails and the White Widow; and how Mr. Silk had acted as the go-between, offering the coyote feral money and a position of power in the city once the war was won. The Spinning Man had always planned for Johnny to infiltrate Caw's allies and turn them against him.

Caw felt stupid—he'd fallen for it all so easily. But then, so had everyone else.

In return, Caw told Selina how he'd looked out for her in the hospital, and how guilty he'd been feeling ever since that night on the roof of her mother's apartment. "I never got the chance to say thank you," he said, turning to her as they whipped through the air, side by side. "You stepped in front of a bullet for me."

"I'd say we're even now," said Selina. Her face darkened. "I know she tried to shoot you. But she's still my mother, you know? No matter what she did."

Caw didn't know what to say. He thought of Cynthia Davenport locked in a cell in the psychiatric hospital, her mind utterly gone.

"We'll visit her together," he said. "When all this is over."

Selina smiled gratefully. "Yeah, I'd like that—thank you." She looked ahead. "Uh-oh."

They were above the park now and could see that the railings were surrounded by police cars. More were pulling up at the gates, and cops with flashlights and guns were moving between the trees. Caw directed his crows to descend at the far side, where it was completely dark. They landed and then the crows lifted away into the trees.

Caw heard shouts of "Freeze!" and "Hands up!" in the distance. He pulled Selina aside as a panther came slinking through the bushes toward them. Caw was about to summon the crows when the big cat tripped over its own feet and landed heavily on the grass. A tranquilizer dart protruded from its dark fur. The panther's eyes closed as its flank rose and fell with slow, steady breaths.

Suddenly Caw was blinded by light and two cops appeared in front of them. "Don't move!" said one. "Hands behind your heads."

Caw held his crows back. He and Selina raised their hands and the cops approached slowly. But just as one grabbed Caw's wrist, a voice called out, "Leave them!" And another man rushed through the trees to their side.

It was Mr. Strickham, wearing a bulletproof vest and a long overcoat.

"Are you sure, sir?" asked the cop holding on to Caw's wrist.

"They're not criminals," said Lydia's dad angrily.

The cops stepped back, and Mr. Strickham beckoned at Caw and Selina to follow him. He looked tired but determined as he led them through the trees, to the fountain at the very center of Blackstone Park. Police officers swarmed all around, and Caw saw that most of the convict ferals were in handcuffs or being treated for injuries on the ground. His heart sank as he saw dead animals lying everywhere—foxes, rats, birds, and more. The bison was sprawled across a bench with blood dripping from its snout while two police officers stood guard. It was a devastating scene.

"This will take some explaining," said Mr. Strickham grimly. "And the press aren't going to hold back. I don't suppose you want to fill me in?"

Caw looked around, but he couldn't see any of his friends among the ferals being arrested. Had they managed to escape?

Caw, squawked Glum from a branch above. *We've found the others—east wall of the park.*

Mr. Strickham looked up. "One of yours, I suppose?"

Caw nodded.

"I guess I should be happy," said Mr. Strickham. "It seems that all the escaped convicts are accounted for." He paused, and Caw saw he was almost overwhelmed with emotion. "If you see my wife and Lydia before I do, tell them . . . tell them I'll see them at home."

One of the cops came running up. "Sir, there's some sort of huge bird over there. We think it's an eagle!"

Mr. Strickham sighed. "Nothing would surprise me tonight." He turned to Caw, his voice businesslike. "Now scram, you two. No more loitering in the park. Got it?"

"Got it," Selina and Caw said in unison.

As they headed toward the east wall, Caw caught sight of Lugmann staring from a cage in the back of a police van. The convict threw himself at the mesh, making it shudder. "You!" he shouted. "Come here! I'll rip you apart! I'll—"

But his shouts were muffled as an officer slammed the door shut. Caw turned away.

They crossed the shadowy grass, leaving the glare of the police lights behind them. Caw saw a moth fluttering on the ground, trying to take flight. One of its wings was broken. He stooped and picked it up, glancing around into the trees.

"Mr. Silk?" said Selina.

Caw realized he hadn't seen his old enemy being arrested with the other convicts. Was he watching them right now?

"Perhaps," he said. "But he's on his own—he's powerless." Caw held open his palm and the moth fluttered into the air, flying lop-sidedly away. "Let's find the others."

At last they came across a group of ferals crowded beneath the east wall. Lydia sat with her back against the wall, her face deathly pale. Mrs. Strickham was kneeling at her side, tending to a wound on her daughter's arm. As Caw began to run toward them, some of the other ferals looked up, and Pip cried out, "It's Caw!"

Racklen caught hold of Caw's arm as he passed. "She's all right," he said. "One of Lugmann's panthers clawed her arm, but she'll be fine."

Mrs. Strickham's eyes widened as Caw approached, but then he realized she was staring past him at Selina, who had hung back, as if afraid.

"The Spinning Man is gone," Caw said.

"Can that be true?" said Madeleine. In the branch above her, squirrels began to squeal in excitement.

With an effort, Lydia smiled up at Caw. "You killed him, didn't you?"

Caw nodded. "For good this time." He turned and gestured for Selina to come closer. Hugging herself nervously, she stepped among the ferals.

"I know you might not trust me," she said, "but . . ."

As Mrs. Strickham stood up and walked over to her, Selina seemed to lose the power of speech. Caw had a moment of panic.

But then Mrs. Strickham took Selina's hand gently and turned to the others. "We all need to learn a thing or two about trust," she said, and glanced at Caw. "We were taken in by our enemies. And when we broke our faith with one another, they almost prevailed."

Racklen lowered his gaze. "I'm sorry, Caw," he said. "We should never have doubted you."

Caw felt odd with the huge man practically bowing in front of him. "It's okay. I know why you did," he said. He thought about Black Corvus and how his own beliefs had been shattered.

Lydia came to her mother's side and leaned against her, clutching the bandage over her injured arm. A pigeon zipped past, cooing, and Crumb stepped out of the crowd. "Police heading this way," he said. "We need to go."

As animals and ferals began to scramble up the wall and slip away into the trees, Mrs. Strickham and Crumb stayed by Caw. "It's good to have you back, Caw," said the pigeon feral.

"It's good to be back," said Caw. He smiled, and Crumb smiled too.

"We must find my husband," said Mrs. Strickham. "I have a feeling he'll be furious about all this."

Caw shook his head. "I've got a message from him. He said he'd see you at home. He said . . . he said he loved you both very much."

For a moment, Mrs. Strickham looked as though she were about to cry. Then she drew herself up and smiled, and Caw saw her arm tighten around Lydia. "Thank you, Caw," she said.

"I'll see you soon, okay?" said Lydia. "*Really* soon, please."

"I promise," said Caw.

Lydia and her mother hurried off between the trees with Crumb, followed by foxes. It was only when they were out of earshot that Selina muttered in a low voice, "Mr. Strickham didn't really say that, did he?"

"No," replied Caw, "but I think it's what he meant."

19

It took two days to salvage the wreck that was Caw's house. It wasn't just the spiders' webs covering every room—the harder Caw looked, the more damage he found. But with Lydia, Selina, Crumb, and Pip helping out, they'd made steady progress. Ali had brought around paint and brushes, and Zeah and Madeleine had rehung the front door on its hinges and replaced Caw's bedroom door entirely. Racklen had removed several Jeep loads of rubbish, including the charred remains of the tree house nest. Caw was surprised that he hadn't felt sorry to see it go. But he realized that it was a past he didn't need to hold on to anymore.

"There!" said Lydia, climbing down from a stepladder by Caw's bedroom window. Her arm was still bandaged from the panther attack. "What do you think?"

She'd hung a pair of curtains on the rail above it—they were blue, with white polar bears dancing across them. Apparently they'd been hers when she was younger.

"I kind of like them," said Caw, putting down his loaded paint-brush. He drew them back, letting sunlight into the room. Glum and Shimmer were perched on the ledge outside.

Couldn't you get drapes with crows on them? said Shimmer.

Caw felt a pang of grief. "That's exactly what Screech would have said."

Glum's beak hung sadly to one side.

I miss him, said Shimmer.

"He's with Milky now," said Caw.

Glum bobbed his head. *Probably annoying him too,* he said cheerfully. Caw smiled and thought of the white crow he had seen in the forest, the ghostly form of Screech. One day he would see his companion again.

Footsteps sounded, coming up the stairs. "Okay, okay," Selina was saying. "Just wait a minute."

She ran into the room, laughing. "Pip wants to show you his trick," she said. "Come onto the landing."

Caw followed Lydia and Selina out of the room. Instead of her normal black clothing, Selina was wearing a sleeveless blue top with a picture of a tortoise lying on its back on a beach chair and above it the words "Life in the slow lane." It must have belonged to Lydia. He smiled to himself—finally it looked like the two of them were becoming friends.

Pip stood on the stairs below, looking up through the gaps in the banister railings. "Ladies and gentlemen, are you ready?" he said.

"We're ready!" said Lydia.

Pip beamed from ear to ear. "Then witness the amazing contortions of Pip, the mouse talker!"

He slotted an arm through a small gap in the railings, up to his shoulder.

So far, so unimpressive, muttered Glum.

Shush, said Shimmer. *Give the kid a chance.*

Pip pushed his body as far as he could between the vertical wooden posts. Then the mouse feral took a deep breath, swelling his chest and then breathing out slowly. As he did so, his rib cage seemed to depress farther than was natural, almost like it was made of putty. It followed his arm between the railings, then expanded on the other side.

Lydia gasped. "That's amazing, Pip!"

"Wait!" he said, his head still on the other side. "I'm not done yet."

Yeah, he's stuck, said Glum, chuckling.

Pip breathed out deeply again, and Caw had to blink in astonishment as his friend squeezed his head through as well. "Ta-da!" he said. "My mice have been teaching me!"

"Weird," said Selina, wincing a little. "But cool, too!"

"What do you think, Caw?" asked Pip eagerly.

"I think . . . ," Caw began, "I think I'm *jealous.* Why can't I be a mouse feral?"

254

Hey! said Glum, batting Caw's leg with a wing. *I'll remind you of that next time I'm carrying you.*

Pip beamed. "I reckon I could squeeze through a keyhole if I keep trying," he said. "Perhaps we can train together, Caw."

"Of course we—"

A knock at the door interrupted him.

"That'll be Mom and Dad," said Lydia. She checked her watch. "Guess what—the Strickham family is going to the theater tonight. *Together!*"

The joy in her face was clear, and though Caw couldn't have been happier for her, he still felt a wave of loneliness. He would have given anything to see his parents again, even if just for a few minutes.

But it wasn't Mr. and Mrs. Strickham at the door.

"Hope I'm not intruding," said the cat feral.

"Of course not!" said Caw as he came down the staircase.

Felix Quaker wiped his shoes on the mat and stepped inside. "Gosh, it's been a long time since I came here."

"Sorry about the mess," said Caw, indicating the bags of rubbish still waiting to be taken away.

"Not at all," said Quaker. "You'd be surprised to know how little it's changed."

He whipped out a small package from behind his back, neatly wrapped in paper.

"What is it?" said Caw.

"A housewarming gift," said Quaker. "Nothing special, I'm afraid."

Caw tore off the paper and saw a metal tin inside. The words "Finest Earl Grey" were written on it. Quaker fished in his pocket and pulled out a lemon. "I didn't bother to wrap this."

"Erm, thank you!" said Caw as he took the lemon.

Quaker looked a little uncomfortable, shifting from foot to foot. "I tell you what—why don't we have a cup now? There's something I need to talk with you about."

When Caw had brewed the tea—closely overseen by the cat feral—Felix, Caw, Lydia, and Selina sat around the dining room table. The Carmichaels' house was no longer the feral headquarters, and the other ferals had returned to their homes. This house belonged to Caw again.

Quaker held his mug in both hands, staring intently into its depths.

"I wanted to talk to you—about the Dark Summer," he said, "and about the Midnight Stone."

Caw sipped his drink. The weight of the cat feral's words hung between them.

"You have it still?" said Quaker.

"It's safe," said Caw. "I swore a vow, remember?"

Quaker nodded. "Your mother vowed to keep it safe, too."

He spoke the words evenly with no hint of accusation, but still Caw bristled. And suddenly he remembered the scene that he had witnessed in his vision, after the white spider bit him in the library. "I saw something in a dream," he said. "A clearing in the woods— my mother, but younger, showing the stone to the Spinning Man."

Quaker's eyebrows lifted a fraction. "You know, then."

Caw shook his head. "I don't really understand."

Felix gazed at him for a moment, then said, "You're ready for the truth, I think."

"Tell me," said Caw. "I've had enough of lies."

The cat feral sipped his tea thoughtfully and then began.

"Very well. You never met your grandfather, did you, Caw? He died before you were born. Your mother was around sixteen or seventeen at the time, I remember. On his deathbed, he told her what she would become, and he gave the Midnight Stone to her. He told her to guard it always." He paused, blowing on his steaming tea. "But his mind was clouding over, and he never told her the most important thing of all—to tell no one else about the stone. Elizabeth had a close friend, and his name was Gideon. Gideon Marshall. She confided in him. She had no one else to tell, and I'm sure she was lonely."

Caw suddenly realized where Quaker was going with the story, and his throat felt tight. "He was the spider feral, wasn't he?"

Felix cocked his head. "Gideon didn't know his parents because he was abandoned as a baby. But what is certain is that one of them was the spider feral. And when he assumed his powers as a boy, the feral community took pity on him, your mother and grandfather most of all. It was the greatest mistake they ever made."

"He became the Spinning Man," whispered Selina.

Quaker nodded. "Years later, when you were born, Caw, Gideon came to your mother. He said he would take care of the Midnight Stone—he said it was too much of a burden with you to look after as well. She refused, but from that day onward it was only a matter of time. Gideon Marshall became deranged and power hungry. He had to have the Midnight Stone. He amassed allies and eventually he struck, and that was the Dark Summer."

Caw sighed heavily. "Why didn't you tell me this before?" he asked.

"Because I promised *never* to tell you," said Quaker. "In the height of the Dark Summer, when it looked like we would lose, your mother made me promise." He looked at Caw, his eyes brimming with tears. "She was ashamed of her terrible part in it, poor Lizzie. So today, I have broken a vow too."

Caw let it all sink in, and Lydia rested a hand on his back. "Are you all right?" she asked gently.

"I think so," he said. Pushing back his chair, he walked away from the table.

"Caw?" said Selina.

"Just give me a minute," he said. "Glum, Shimmer. I need you."

He went straight out of the back door, determination hardening in his heart. The crows followed him.

Caw pointed up at the tree. "Bring it," he said.

What are you going to do? said Shimmer.

"Please, just do it," said Caw.

She took off, flying into the blackened branches as Caw drew the Crow's Beak from its sheath.

Shimmer returned with the Midnight Stone clutched in her talons. She dropped it on the ground.

Caw? said Glum.

He gazed at the jet-black stone in front of him. How could something so small have caused so much sorrow? It had pitted feral against feral; it had shed the blood of countless innocents.

My mother, my father, Screech.

Gideon Marshall and Cynthia Davenport.

How many others he'd never even known the names of? And for what? So that one man's soul could prevail. Black Corvus had wanted to live forever, and that wish had rippled through the centuries, becoming a crashing wave that swept onward and destroyed people's lives.

Until now.

Caw sensed that the others had gathered by the kitchen window.

He didn't care if they saw. He held the Crow's Beak high above the Midnight Stone.

He didn't care about the vow Black Corvus had sworn.

He had never sworn that vow.

Caw was the crow talker, descendant of Black Corvus, but he was also much more than that. And he had seen enough horror.

It ended here.

He looked back to the window briefly and nodded to his friends. Then, with a grunt of effort, he brought the blade down on the stone as hard as he could.

There was no flash of light. No great earthquake. Caw felt nothing more than the reverberation of the impact through his wrist. When he looked down, he saw the Midnight Stone had been smashed into several pieces. He sheathed his sword, closed his eyes, and sent out a summons. In seconds, a murder of crows had landed in the garden.

"Take a piece each," he said. "Fly away from the city and drop them. It doesn't matter where—I don't want to know."

One by one, the crows flew in, scooping up small fragments and flapping away in different directions. Jack Carmichael watched them disappear into the distance.

Then he turned and walked slowly back to his home.

RAISED BY CROWS.
HUNTED BY DARKNESS.

Don't miss a single page of
this epic fantasy series!